"I don't want you to touch me!"

Rebecca backed away from him as she added, "I'm beginning to believe that being pawed by one's employer is mandatory for women."

Byron replied coldly, "I'm not so desperate to get a woman into my bed that I have to pay one. This job is purely and simply to look after my daughter's needs. Not mine. If you think I'm taking advantage of you, perhaps you should look to yourself for possible causes. Maybe you're not giving off the right, shall we say, vibes?"

"Are you implying—" Rebecca spluttered angrily.

"Last night, Rebecca, your response was somewhat exuberant, you can't deny that. You should be thanking me from the bottom of your maidenly heart for not taking what was so willingly offered!"

D0951594

Lynsey Stevens, an Australian author, has a sense of humor that adds a lively quality to her writing. She has always enjoyed her work as a librarian—in a modern library providing children's activities, puppets, theater and other community services—but her first love is writing. Though her earlier attempts at writing historical and adventure were unsuccessful, and her first romance novel was rejected, Lynsey now has several published books to her credit. And she hints at the presence of a real live Harlequin hero in her life.

Books by Lynsey Stevens

HARLEQUIN ROMANCE

HARLEQUIN PRESENTS

Don't miss any of our special offers. Write to us at the following address for information on our newest releases.

Harlequin Reader Service
901 Fuhrmann Blvd., P.O. Box 1397, Buffalo, NY 14240
Canadian address: P.O. Box 603,
Fort Erie, Ont. L2A 5X3

But Never Love

Lynsey Stevens

Harlequin Books

TORONTO • NEW YORK • LONDON
AMSTERDAM • PARIS • SYDNEY • HAMBURG
STOCKHOLM • ATHENS • TOKYO • MILAN

Original hardcover edition published in 1988
by Mills & Boon Limited

ISBN 0-373-02988-8

Harlequin Romance first edition June 1989

CHAPTER ONE

REBECCA'S heartbeats quickened. She was almost home. The break in the mallee trees indicated the way in to the farm, and she turned her smart pale orange Laser off the road, the tyres crunching on the loose gravel as the car rocked over the corrugations.

The headlights flashed on the newly whitewashed gateposts, the neatly painted sign. Bay Ridge. Rebecca's eyebrows rose. Jock had had the sign fixed. When she'd left it had been hanging crookedly by one corner, and had done so for a couple of years. No one seemed to get around to rehanging it.

She headed slowly up the driveway, her lights making a tunnel in the dark blackness created by the avenue of pine branches meeting overhead to block out the lighter night sky. The trees stopped short of the house and, slowing the car, she drew to a halt in front of the garden gate. The car's lights flowed over the well-remembered area, momentarily illuminating the sturdy house and its surroundings. The old, slightly askew wooden shed had been replaced by a much bigger, far more modern building, and she saw that the garden hedge had been clipped, another job Jock had never found time to do before Rebecca left.

But her eyes were drawn to the house, its solid shape an outline in the blackness, and her heart sank when she realised it was in darkness. She opened the door and climbed out of the car to stand with her eyes fixed on the house that had been her home for the first twenty years of her life.

And now she was finally here, she was as unsure of her welcome as she was of her reason for returning. Coming home had seemed the perfect solution. But the old problems were still here, weren't they? Rebecca sighed.

Rudy would be pleased to see her, and she him. But what about Jock? Jock, her grandfather, was such an autocrat, determined and stubborn. He was a man of steel and expected everyone to fall in with his plans, his orders, Rudy and herself.

Jock's sparse letters usually reproached her for leaving the island, but lately he had mellowed. Or had that been her imagination? Perhaps she had read a softening in her grandfather's letters because she'd wanted it to be that way. At least she hadn't imagined the fact that he had been writing more frequently these past months.

But now she was here she began to have definite doubts about Jock's reception of her sudden appearance. They had had a dreadful row before she'd left, a row to outshine their previous arguments, and there had been plenty of those.

In Sydney it had all seemed so simple, just to go home. Rebecca sighed again. What was that old saying? Never go back.

And two years ago, in the heat of that argument, she'd sworn she'd never return, not for all the opals in Coober Pedy.

Uncertainty niggled at her, tightening her stomach. Would she really be forgiven after all this time?

She was glad she'd kept in touch with her family, even though that first letter from Adelaide had been difficult to write, had taken her over a week to compose. And she'd been so relieved when, a few letters on, her grandfather had written back. They were family, after all.

Even Rudy had despatched an intermittent rambling note or two in which he'd complained bitterly about being tied to the farm, the isolation of life on Kangaroo

Island, the drudgery of working long, hard hours with Jock. He'd said she was lucky to have escaped. Actually, she hadn't heard from Rudy in ages. But then, he wasn't a letter-writer.

A small frown furrowed her brow. *Had* it been a mistake to come back? She swallowed nervously. Her decision to return had been a spontaneous, spur-of-the-moment thing. At least, her actual departure had been. However, for the past few months, thoughts of home and her family had been foremost in her mind. The idea of returning to the island and Bay Ridge had been steadily growing.

Her overnight case carrying her essentials was on the seat beside her, and she reached in and lifted it out of the car. The rest of her gear—most of her worldly goods, she grimaced wryly—was in the back of the car, and she could leave it there until the morning.

She walked hesitantly across to the gate, picking her way carefully in the almost-blackness of the night. To her surprise the gate swung on well-oiled hinges. It used to squeak frightfully, she recalled.

Her eyes were accustomed to the darkness now, and she walked on the path towards the house. Three steps up on to the veranda that ran the length of the front of the house. Across the weathered cement to the front door. Raising her hand, she gave a tentative knock that seemed softer than the thudding of her heart.

Rebecca resolutely stiffened her back and knocked louder. No one came. She set down her case and put her hand on the doorknob. It turned in her fingers and she pushed the door open. Soft light came from the living-room on her left. Whoever was still out of bed must have drawn the heavy curtains across the windows, shutting out the windy night.

'Hello.' Her voice sounded hollow and husky. 'Anyone home? Jock? Rudy?'

She stepped into the hallway and was immediately aware of the warmth after the chill of the wind outside.

'Hello,' she called again, and moved towards the dull pool of light that escaped through the living-room doorway.

A chair creaked and footsteps crossed the carpeted floor. Then a tall figure appeared in the doorway, filling it completely, softly outlined by the light.

Rebecca stopped, her eyes widening. 'Rudy!' She flung herself at him. In three steps she was on him, her arms going around his neck, her lips moving against his cheek.

'Oh, Rudy! It's good to see you. To be back.'

Even as she said it, some part of her brain was registering a protest. Facts were being processed and weren't quite adding up. Rudy was tall and broad. But was he as tall as . . .? And his shoulders, did she remember them being quite so broad?

A tangy aftershave teased her nostrils as her fingers ran over the soft cotton of a light shirt that didn't begin to disguise the mound of masculine muscle beneath. Strong arms had wrapped firmly around her back, and her legs came up against long, taut, denim-clad thighs.

The arms tightened, and some almost imperceptible change in the timbre of the embrace had her stiffening. She pulled backwards, as far as the encircling bands of steel would allow her to, and her eyes widened. His face was backlit and her eyes strained in the semi-darkness to pick out the man's features, searching for reassurance. A cold finger of dread ran up her spine.

'You're not . . .' Her voice faltered and died.

'Rudy?' came the deep, resonant query. 'No, I'm afraid not. I could almost wish I was.'

'Who...who are you?' she got out, her hands pushing ineffectively against his shoulders, for he held her fast with seemingly little effort.

'As Rudy isn't here,' he said, ignoring her breathless question, 'maybe I should welcome you back in his place.'

His voice had dropped, was liquid gold playing a sensuous tune on her nerve-endings, filling her with a sudden inexplicable excitement she was unable to suppress. She'd never heard a voice so deeply intriguing, so full of vibrant male sensuality. Almost mesmerised, she made no move to resist the lips that slowly came downwards.

His mouth was cool and firm and stirred teasingly on hers. But it was only a momentary taunt, for the first touch ignited a flame that became a fire, growing in intensity as his lips moved hungrily, tantalisingly over her mouth.

Time and place ceased to exist, and reason so readily, so very rapidly, deserted her. She found herself returning his kiss as though compelled to do so. Her response, sparked initially by his virile voice, was fanned by the heady masculine scent of him, the firm feel of hard muscle, alive in every fibre of her body.

Of its own accord her body arched against his, her full breasts crushed to his rock-hard chest, the muscles of her thighs tensing as the thin gaberdine of her slacks and the denim of his jeans seemed to be no barrier between their lower bodies. They couldn't get closer to each other.

Tiny curls of pleasure rose in ever-increasing waves from the pit of her stomach, and her heartbeats began to pound inside her. Or were they his heartbeats? There seemed to be no separation, for in unison they beat a thunderous tattoo.

Large hands stirred erotically over her back, sliding down to her hips to draw her impossibly closer, only accelerating her arousal. When his lips finally surrendered hers they were both breathless.

Rebecca's hands had somehow found their way around his neck, her fingers twined in the soft, thick strands of his hair, and in the semi-darkness the brilliant blaze of his eyes stole away what little of her breath remained. She trembled and swallowed convulsively. What was she doing, she asked herself, making love to a complete stranger? It was utter madness. Kissing him as though...

Her whole body stilled then, poised, as a shocked awareness turned her suddenly cold. How could she have behaved the way she had? She had kissed this stranger with an insinuating intimacy she hadn't known she was capable of, without a thought about what he would think of her.

She felt her knees tremble and knew he must be aware of it, for they were still moulded together. What must he be thinking of her? That she was thoroughly uninhibited, that he was undoubtedly on to a good thing. What a laugh, she chastised herself bitterly. There wasn't much else he could think of her after the last few minutes.

And she was still standing locked in his arms, far closer to him than she'd been to any man before, for their union seemed somehow more than purely physical. Rebecca drew on her failing strength, and her hands moved down to push against his chest, her fingers still registering the heady sensation of the feel of firm muscles.

But his arms held her fast and her eyes widened, flying up to lock with his, a faint breath of fear curling inside her. Then one corner of his mouth lifted fractionally and he slowly released her.

Without the support of his tall frame, she thought her numb body would crumple and fall, but somehow she managed to stay upright, even if she did have to quell a sudden urge to be held close to him again, feel his strength, the thunderous excitement of his kiss. She lowered her gaze in case he should see her body's duplicity in her eyes.

To her mortification, her voice had caught painfully in her throat and her hands were beginning to ache where they were clasped tightly together behind her back. The last thing she wanted him to see was their violent trembling.

She knew she should laugh, say something witty, treat it all as a joke and bring some perspective back into the situation. So sorry, I thought you were my brother. Ha, ha! But she just couldn't. For that kiss had hardly been light-hearted. Perhaps it had started out that way, but the moment their lips had met...

She'd never responded to a kiss quite so unrestrainedly. She'd always remained coolly in command. So where was the so poised, so self-assured, always so self-contained Ms Rebecca Grainger now?

The tall body standing before her moved and she tensed, but he was only shifting slightly so that he could rest his shoulder easily against the wall, hooking one thumb into the waistband of his jeans, long legs crossing one bare foot over the other. He broke the silence at last.

'I guess we should introduce ourselves, although a mundane "how do you do" will seem something of an anti-climax, don't you think?' There was a note of wry humour in the deep voice that continued to play over Rebecca with that same inciting awareness. 'I'm Byron Willoughby.'

Rebecca gazed at his outstretched hand and then slowly put her hand in his, where it was immediately lost as his fingers closed around hers. He didn't attempt to prolong the contact, and when he released her her fingers continued to tingle elatedly.

The light from the living-room highlighted one side of his face now, and he raised an eyebrow enquiringly, waiting for her to speak.

'I'm Rebecca,' she told him, and he repeated the name softly, enquiringly, sending a shiver teasingly up her spine. She raised her chin and drew a steadying breath. 'Rebecca Grainger,' she elaborated, with a little more self-possession this time.

Byron Willoughby seemed to tense, and then he pushed himself upright, his eyes not leaving her face. 'You're Becca?'

Becca. It was two years since anyone had called her that, and she gazed at him in surprise. Jock must have mentioned her.

'I suppose you work here?' she asked, wishing she could read his expression, for she sensed a stillness in him, a sudden watchfulness.

'You could say that,' he replied after a lengthy moment. 'Shall we go into the living-room?' He motioned towards the doorway.

On stiff legs Rebecca moved through the doorway, and another surprise awaited her. The room was large and comfortable and homey, as she remembered it, but drastic changes had been made. The furniture had been rearranged, the book-shelves and the grandfather clock changing walls, the lounge chairs repositioned. And that dark, woodgrained, roll-topped desk was new. There was a different air about the room.

But then, why not? she asked herself. After all, it was two years since she'd touched a polishing cloth to the family heirlooms, she reminded herself wryly. Why shouldn't Jock make a few changes?

Her gaze shifted to the fireplace. Where was Jock's favourite chair? She'd never imagined he'd get rid of the old-fashioned eyesore. It was part of him somehow, that faded, overstuffed lounger that always stood by the fireplace. She could just about see Jock in it now, warming his feet on the fender.

A new leather chair stood in the place of Jock's old one. And that was obviously where Byron Willoughby had been sitting when she'd disturbed him, for an open magazine lay on the floor beside the chair, as though it had slipped from his fingers when he'd stood up. There were more magazines, issues on farming, she noticed, piled on the small coffee-table, and an empty coffee mug stood beside the magazines.

The stranger must have been catching up on farming methods. Jock had certainly picked the right man; not only did he look capable of handling any job, no matter how physically taxing, but he was conscientious as well. She glanced down at her wristwatch, surprised at the lateness of the hour.

'I didn't realise the time. The *Troubridge* docked a little late this evening. We had a stiff south-easterly all the way.' The sturdy vehicular ferry had been heading into a thirty-knot-plus gale from Port Adelaide for the one-hundred-and-forty-kilometre trip down through St Vincent Gulf, across Backstairs Passage to Kangaroo Island. The very rough voyage had taken over seven hours, and some of the passengers had had a wretched trip. 'I suppose Jock and Rudy are in bed?'

'Did Jock know you were coming?' Byron Willoughby asked, motioning her to the chair opposite the new leather one.

Rebecca felt a spurt of irritation that he should be playing host. Almost as if he owned the place.

She sat down, watching as he lowered himself lithely into the lounger, crossing one denim-clad leg over the knee of the other, his hands resting along the arms of the chair.

Her eyes ran over him, reassessing him in the improved light. Probably in his early thirties, she guessed, and he was no less handsome, she had to admit, now that she could see him properly. Her senses stirred again and she stiffened, feeling as though every muscle in her body had flexed, waiting.

His dark hair was a little long but sat tidily, clean and thickly lustrous, the front swept across his forehead above straight, dark eyebrows. His eyes, too, looked dark, although she couldn't be sure from this distance. And when she'd been close to him, with his arms around

her, the colour of his eyes had been the very last thing
on her mind. Those moments had been purely sensation. Her body responded to her thoughts and she
quickly forced that scene from her mind, the line of her
full lips tightening.

His facial features were slightly craggy, she decided,
and his jaw was firm and square, suggesting a forceful
nature. On his cheekbone below his left eye he had a
scar about an inch long which somehow added rather
than detracted from his rugged good looks. Rebecca
wondered how he'd got the scar. An accident? Or
perhaps a fight? He looked like the type who could
handle himself in any tight corner. But he had a nice
mouth. A very nice mouth. And cool, caressing lips.

Her eyes skimmed hurriedly downwards. The long,
tanned column of his throat disappeared in to the open
neck of his checked cotton shirt, the rolled-up sleeves
snugly fitting the well-developed muscles in his forearms.
Square, broad shoulders, muscular chest tapering to a
narrow waist. Her gaze dropped lower over his legs to
his bare feet. Nice, well-shaped feet.

Rebecca swallowed and returned her gaze to his face.
One corner of his mouth lifted in quizzical amusement,
as though he was totally aware of her appraisal, and to
her embarrassment she felt hot colour wash her face. He
raised one dark eyebrow again, and she realised with a
start that he was waiting for her to answer his question.

'I'm sorry. I beg your pardon?' she managed to get
out.

'I said, did Jock know you were coming?' he repeated.

Rebecca shook her head. 'No,' she replied slowly.
'It's . . . I wanted to surprise him,' she added. There was
no need for this man to know all the gory details, what
had precipitated her flight from Bay Ridge, or why she'd
decided to return after all this time.

'I understood you haven't been——' he paused slightly
'—back for some time.'

'Not for a couple of years,' Rebecca told him, feeling for some reason just a little defensive. 'I've been working on the mainland. Now I've come home.' She raised her chin unconsciously.

'And how long is it since you heard from Jock?'

Rebecca shrugged. 'We're neither of us regular letter writers, but he wrote just last week, actually.'

He held her gaze levelly. 'Your arrival *will* be a surprise,' Byron Willoughby said softly. 'I think Jock might have appreciated some forewarning.' His dark eyes continued to hold hers.

Did she sense a note of censure in his tone? What right had he to criticise? She felt a revival of anger, not helped by the fact that she knew what he said was the truth. But she'd decided on the spur of the moment to return to the island and home.

The day after she'd received the letter from Jock asking her when her annual leave was due and would she like to spend her holiday at Bay Ridge, she had had another confrontation with her new boss. With Bay Ridge in mind she'd resigned on the spot, packed her things and left Sydney.

And why shouldn't she come home? She was still Jock's granddaughter. Yes, perhaps she *should* have let Jock know she was returning. But she didn't want this stranger telling her that.

'Jock's my grandfather, and I know he'll be pleased to see me,' she stated with far more authority than she actually felt.

Byron Willoughby made no comment, but continued to regard her with his steady gaze until she began to wonder if he was aware of her fiery parting from Jock.

So what if he was? Suddenly she felt tired as a wave of fatigue washed over her. Was it any wonder? she asked herself. She had been on the move for days—long, exhausting hours of driving across the country—and now she was home, at her journey's end. She smothered a yawn.

'I'm sorry. I guess my travelling has caught up with me. I think perhaps I should have a shower and go to bed. I won't disturb Jock tonight.'

'Do you want something to eat? Some coffee?'

Rebecca shook her head. 'No, thanks. I had a snack on the ferry.'

After a moment the man opposite her stood up. 'I'll get your cases for you,' he said easily.

'My small overnight bag will do for tonight.' Rebecca stood up too. 'I left it at the door. The rest of my stuff can wait until the morning.'

Switching on the hall light, Byron Willoughby walked out to the door and returned with her bag.

Rebecca led the way through to the bedroom next to the living-room and stopped, turning to look at him, her hand on the doorknob. 'Do you know if the bed's made up in my room?'

'All the beds are made up,' he said, and she held out her hand for her case.

'Thank you.'

He slowly released the bag.

'Perhaps I'll see you tomorrow.' Rebecca swung the door open. 'I hope I haven't kept you up.'

He shook his head, looked as though he was about to say something and then changed his mind. Nodding a curt goodnight, he turned back towards the living-room.

Rebecca's eyes followed him, and then she shrugged slightly and switched on the bedroom light. She was filled with an overwhelming relief that at least her bedroom was still the same, the single bed with its slightly faded pink chenille spread, the old dressing-table, even the furry rug on the floor.

She sighed gratefully and pulled her nightgown and toiletries from her bag. Outside in the hall again she saw that the living-room light was still burning, so she set off in the opposite direction and turned the corner towards the bathroom, tiptoeing so that she wouldn't wake Jock, who slept in the room across from the bathroom at the back of the house. Rudy's room was opposite hers, and she knew from past experience that nothing short of an atomic bomb blast would wake her brother when he was asleep.

The hot shower relaxed her tired muscles, and she felt wonderfully refreshed as she returned to her room and crawled thankfully between the sheets. Her bones seemed to melt into the comfortable mattress she remembered so well. Things didn't look quite so bad. Jock would be pleased to see her, she told herself as she snuggled down into the bed. She and Rudy were the only family he had left.

Rebecca closed her eyes and, unbidden, a dark, craggy face appeared before her. She shivered slightly as she recalled those two strong arms around her and her unrestrained response to his kiss.

It was all merely a mistake. She had mistaken Byron Willoughby for Rudy, and when she'd discovered he wasn't her brother that kiss had.... Well, it was plain, simple surprise that had made her respond. Wasn't it? He'd taken her unawares. She shifted irritatedly in the bed. In the morning it would all seem like a joke. She'd laugh about it. And so would Byron Willoughby.

Byron Willoughby. Had she heard that name before somewhere? Her mind searched about without success. No, she couldn't think. Maybe she was mistaken again. Perhaps it was just that his was an unusual name. Byron Willoughby. A name out of a romantic novel. She smiled to herself, amused at the thought. Byron Willoughby, the tall, dark and handsome hero. He *was* tall, dark and handsome. Even if he had taken advantage of her. She smiled sleepily. That was pure romantic fiction, too.

CHAPTER TWO

THE house was quiet when Rebecca awoke, and she stretched languidly. She'd slept better than she had in ages. When she glanced at her wristwatch her eyes widened in surprise. It was almost eleven o'clock. My God! She'd all but slept the clock around.

Thrusting back the covers, she slid out of bed, stopping as she spied her two larger suitcases just inside the door. Someone had brought them in while she was sleeping. Her throat went dry and she swallowed, her cheeks growing hot at the thought of Byron Willoughby seeing her asleep, vulnerable somehow.

What was wrong with her? She mentally shook herself. It was probably Rudy who'd carried her cases inside anyway. She crossed the room and, opening one case, drew out fresh underclothes, jeans and a light sweater.

She shivered as she dressed, listening to the wind outside. The thick walls of the sturdy house kept the elements at bay, but the sound of the wind, which seemed not to have abated, reminded Rebecca of her trip across to the island.

Once dressed, she walked across to stand before the mirror to brush her hair. She paused, her eyes assessing herself. She'd changed since she left home. She could see that in a glance. She'd fined down, and there was a little more maturity in her features.

Her nose was small and straight, with a slight uptilt, her lips full and well-shaped, and she'd been told she had good cheekbones, whatever that meant, she grimaced wryly. She tilted her head. She had a somewhat determined chin, a feature she had definitely inherited from Jock.

She pulled the brush through her dark hair, which she wore longer now, almost reaching her shoulders, and it fell in loose, natural curls. Her figure had improved, too, she thought mockingly. She'd lost about ten pounds and she knew she looked better for it. Her breasts were high and firm, her waist narrow with slim, almost boyish hips, and her legs were long and shapely.

Her brush faltered midstroke and her shoulders drooped a little. A slow sigh escaped her. Yet what had she really accomplished in the two years she'd been away? If she was honest, she'd have to admit that the freedom she'd craved when she left Kangaroo Island had turned sour on her. Oh, she'd had a good time, sown her wild oats, if only mild ones.

And she'd made a success of her job, been promoted quickly to the prestigious position of personal assistant to one of the directors. Her salary had risen accordingly, and she'd indulged herself with the small car and a better apartment.

But she'd begun to realise her life had no meaning. In the midst of a loud and laughing party one could be lonely. And the actions of her new boss hadn't helped at all. Men could be so... She shook her head and her eyes searched her face.

Had the two years she'd spent away from Bay Ridge been worth it? She pulled a face at herself. Well, she hadn't met any handsome millionaires and been swept off her feet to the exotic playgrounds of the jet-set. Her lips quirked wryly without amusement.

In fact, she hadn't met a man she'd fancied, rich or poor. There had been plenty of men in the social whirl, but not that special one for her. Rebecca sighed. Maybe she was one of those women who never met her soul-mate.

For some inexplicable reason her thoughts swung immediately to Byron Willoughby, and she blinked unseeingly at her reflection. A tantalising quiver rose from the depths of her stomach. She could almost feel his arms about her, his lips moving on hers. And she knew a gnawing desire to experience that intoxicating sensation again.

Expelling the breath she held in an ejaculation of exasperation, she threw her brush on to the dressing-table and turned away from the mirror. She had to be mad, she told herself. She'd met him less than twenty-four hours ago, they'd kissed quite by accident, and now she was imagining she was attracted to him.

Rebecca shook her head. It was all part and parcel of a stage she must be going through. Her emotions were off balance, what with Paul Drewett, her ex-boss, and coming home. Upset sensitivities. Yes, a stage in her life.

The sexual stage? she asked herself disparagingly. Sex. Or perhaps old-fashioned lust. Last night with Byron Willoughby had quite simply been a carry-over from the temptation of taking what the handsome Paul Drewett had so plainly offered. Byron's rugged attraction was far more potent than Paul's too-regular good looks, so could she be blamed, after weeks of personal turmoil, for being swayed by that attraction?

But it wasn't quite that somehow... A frown creased her brow. She felt her heartbeats change pace. Byron Willoughby's kisses had—— Oh, stop it! she admonished herself and, pulling the waistband of her sweater over her hips, she strode across the room and opened the door.

She walked through to the kitchen, knowing instinctively by the timbre of the silence that she was alone in the house. And almost immediately she noticed the note propped up against the sugar bowl in the centre of the table. With shaky fingers she picked it up. The bold, flowing script was nothing like her grandfather's spidery handwriting, and she didn't need to glance at the 'B.W.' on the bottom to know who had written the message.

'You were asleep when we left. Jock will be back about lunch time.'

Short and to the point. A man of few words, she reflected as she made herself a cup of tea and some toast to still the grumblings of her empty stomach. She hadn't eaten since the light snack she'd had on board the *Troubridge* the evening before.

Jock and Rudy, and presumably Byron Willoughby, would have had their morning break, but she wouldn't expect them to stop for lunch for an hour. Would her grandfather and her brother have changed much in two years? She swallowed nervously, reminding herself that everything changed. She had.

With her suitcase of clothes disposed of, she made a couple of trips out to her car for the other cartons that held all her things: books she couldn't bear to part with, knick-knacks from her flat. Most of it she'd left behind when she'd decided to come home, when she'd made up her mind there was nothing to stop her just getting in to her car and heading back to South Australia. Nothing and no one. No deep friendships or burning romances. She'd never really looked for a steady relationship. Hadn't she decided to leave all that behind her when she'd left the island?

How would Davie Kelly react when he heard she'd returned? Her lips curled humorously as she imagined him going into a panic. Jock's idea, with the full approval of Davie's parents, had been that she and Davie would suit each other nicely. Rebecca had been simply and totally furious. With her grandfather and with the Kellys.

And hurt had fanned the flame of her anger. In retrospect, her anger was mostly wounded pride, she told herself a little grimly. For Davie's attitude, and the conversation she'd overheard two years ago, had flicked her on the raw at the time. Now she could even laugh at it.

She strolled desultorily back to the kitchen and, opening the back door, she stepped outside and walked past the shelter of the added laundry enclosure. The wind had now died a little, but it still whipped her shoulder-length dark hair back from her face, tangling her curls. The clean, tangy freshness of it on her upturned face restored some of her good humour as she gazed around the well-remembered farmyard.

Jock had certainly spruced the old place up. Everywhere she looked she could see the changes. Fences had been straightened and repaired, grass mown, trees pruned. In fact, she hadn't seen the farm looking so good in years, not since her father's death.

She wandered over to the gate and leant her arms along the top rail, her mind filled nostalgically with years of memories she hadn't known she had stored up inside her. Somehow there had never seemed to be time to think about the past, not until recently, anyway.

The small but prosperous electrical firm she'd worked for in Adelaide had been bought out by a large national company, and as she had been secretary to the owner of the smaller firm she had been asked to go from Adelaide to Sydney with him to the new headquarters. The job had been demanding and thoroughly enjoyable, and when she'd proved her competence within the new company she'd moved quickly up the ladder until, six months ago, she'd been promoted to secretary to one of the directors.

Mr King had been a pleasure to work with, but unfortunately he had suffered a severe heart-attack three months later and been forced to retire. Then things had started to fall apart. She'd been transferred to the position of personal assistant to Paul Drewett, one of the up-and-coming executives of the firm and son of the chairman of the board. Her lips tightened.

Paul Drewett knew he was attractive. He was suave and certainly sophisticated, and he'd made it plain immediately that he wanted more from Rebecca than her secretarial skills.

The fact that he was quite happily and advantageously married to the daughter of one of the other directors didn't seem to bother him. They could have a great time together, he told Rebecca; with no ties, no commitments, affairs like that were the spice of life.

And Rebecca had to acknowledge she'd been tempted. No man had ever come close to making her want to surrender to him completely, and she was beginning to think there was something wrong with her, that what Davie Kelly had said about her was true.

Paul was handsome, exciting. But she recognised that her capitulation would have been for all the wrong reasons. To decide that at twenty-two it was time to lose one's virginity and prove one wasn't frigid wasn't a good enough motive, she'd discovered, to wipe away her former reticence.

So when Paul had issued an ultimatum she had angrily handed in her notice and headed homewards. It was the excuse she'd needed to make the break.

She forced her attention back to the farm. To her right some distance away stood the original home built by the first Grainger to settle on Bay Ridge in the mid-eighteen-hundreds. It had always been kept in good repair, and was often used as quarters for the hired farm hands. Jock's father, Rebecca's great-grandfather, had built the homestead in which they now lived.

Washing flapped on the clothes line behind the old cottage, so Byron Willoughby wasn't the only hand Jock had hired, Rebecca reflected. No wonder the farm looked so prosperous and well kept. But why was Byron Willoughby up at the house? Surely he would have bunked down at the cottage like the other hands. She frowned. Did Jock know him from somewhere? Was that why his name had had that momentarily familiar ring to it? She shrugged. Maybe Jock had made him foreman or something, for him to have special privileges. But where did that leave Rudy? It didn't fit.

The old king mallee grove where she'd played hide and seek with Rudy looked as thick as ever. She smiled, remembering the times they'd used the grove as a fort against attacking Red Indians, or simply as a hideaway when Jock was on the warpath.

Rebecca stirred guiltily. From two years on, things looked so much clearer and appeared in a far different perspective. Somehow she couldn't shake the sudden feeling that she had acted like a spoilt, selfish brat.

The car accident that had claimed her father had been a terrible blow to them all, yet doubly so to Jock, who had not only lost his son but had been suddenly left to manage the entire farm on his own, coupled with having to take the single-handed responsibility of herself, then sixteen, and Rudy, who was a year older. And Jock hadn't been a young man at the time. Today he must be, what? Her grandfather was seventy-eight.

No wonder he needed the strong arms of Rudy and Byron Willoughby to run the farm. Yet, during her adolescence, Jock had seemed nothing short of immortal. But, of course, even Jock grew older.

Rebecca's heart was a heavy weight in her chest. Jock had needed her, too. But she'd run away, and her leaving had added to his burden. In a flash of painful self-revelation she admitted she hadn't even returned for the right reasons. She'd come home because she was bored, jaded by the social whirl, the plastic personalities, the insincerity. She'd have to make it up to Jock somehow. If he let her stay, that was. Who could blame him if he sent her packing?

Shoving her hands into the pockets of her jeans, she strolled back towards the house. Just being here, back at Bay Ridge, was a balm that soothed away the stress that had seemed to hold her perpetually tense of late. If Jock should tell her to go...

Rebecca returned to the kitchen and sat down at the table, resting her chin in the palm of one hand. It felt so right to be here, to be home. She drew a long, satisfying breath, sitting back in her chair, inhaling the familiar scent of the room, the sharp, clean air.

She threaded her fingers slowly through her soft, curling hair, absently pulling one dark tendril, letting it spring back into place.

What had made her unsettled in Sydney? It wasn't just the persistent attentions of Paul. She sighed. Perhaps she'd finally grown up. And with maturity came the gradual realisation that the kind of life she was living left her empty and dissatisfied. She had no close friends, not even her flatmate. There was no time to talk; life was too fast for that.

Her lips twisted cynically and she stood up to prowl around the kitchen, touching this, straightening that, until she realised that the sound intruding into her self-pitying thoughts was a car approaching.

That same face, becoming so easily familiar, swam before her eyes, and her heartbeats fluttered erratically. Would it be Byron Willoughby? Rebecca pulled herself up short. What was this annoying preoccupation she seemed to have with Byron Willoughby? After all, she'd only known him for mere hours, and what was a simple kiss in this enlightened day and age?

Her fingers went unconsciously to touch her mouth as she felt again the pressure of those cool, firm lips moving so provocatively on hers. It was just a kiss, she told herself. Why make such an issue of it? It wasn't as though she'd never been kissed before. She was being ridiculous.

The sound of the car died. Of course, it would be Jock. Rebecca moved towards the door, drawn, but apprehensive. She recognised the old Holden utility at once, dented and rusty. Jock had driven it around the farm and the island for a good fifteen years. For as long as she could remember, the ute had looked as though it was about to fall to pieces. But it just kept on hanging together. Probably because Jock willed it to, she reflected wryly.

Rebecca stepped outside and stopped, watched the figure of her grandfather climb slowly from the cabin and just as slowly straighten. Rebecca's breath caught painfully in her chest. This couldn't be Jock. This man was old. Her grandfather was as tall and as straight as an Australian ghost gum.

The figure standing beside the utility seemed to have shrunk, was just a little stooped, and the once iron-grey hair was completely white. Then he was walking hesitantly towards her. Rebecca felt a rush of tears blur her eyes and she blinked them away.

'Hello, Jock,' she got out tentatively, and he stopped, his eyes roving over her.

He moved his lips but no words came. Then she was in his arms, her sobs breaking from her in a damburst. It was almost as though she was a child again, hurt and seeking solace, and Jock was there as he'd always seemed to be way back then.

'Ah, Becca,' he murmured thickly. 'You came home.'

Her face was buried in the front of his well-washed, checked flanelette shirt that smelled of the farm, the grass, the crops, the fresh earth. Her arms were around him, and she registered that Jock had indeed lost weight. She stood back from him to look worriedly up at him.

Jock smiled crookedly. 'We all grow older, even me,' he said, his voice still slightly unsteady and his eyes bright. His fingers lifted her chin.

'Let's have a look at you.' His gaze roamed over her face. 'Pretty as a picture,' he said softly. 'You always did have a look of your grandmother. She was a beauty, too.'

'Oh, Jock.' Rebecca's voice broke as her fingers covered his. 'It's so good to be home. I don't know why I waited so long. I missed you and Rudy so much, and I didn't realise until I came home how much I love this place.'

A fleeting cloud shadowed Jock's expression and he sighed softly. 'Let's go inside, Becca, and talk.'

She followed him into the house and automatically brewed some tea. Her grandfather loved his cuppa.

Jock sat down at the kitchen table and clasped his gnarled, capable hands together on the table top, not speaking until she'd placed his cup of tea in front of him and joined him, sitting facing him.

'Becca——' he began, and paused.

'Are you pleased to see me?' she had to ask him, and he nodded.

'I've missed you, too, love. Every moment of these past two years,' he said sincerely, and Rebecca smiled.

'You know I was scared stiff you—well, that you wouldn't want to have me back.'

'I never wanted you to go in the beginning. I just——' He shrugged. 'I couldn't say the right thing, and I guess I was a stubborn, pig-headed old man.'

His hands were trembling, and Rebecca covered them with hers. 'I was stubborn and pig-headed, too.' Her eyes fell. 'And pretty selfish. I can see that now. But I didn't want to... I just wasn't ready to settle down as you wanted me to. I felt restricted, as though I'd be spending the rest of my life in one tiny square, never getting to experience more of the whole.' She sighed. 'But I shouldn't have run off the way I did. I guess you must have been worried about the farm, trying to keep it going without Dad, and our rebelliousness, Rudy's and mine, wouldn't have helped.'

'No. Don't go blaming yourself, love. You and Rudy were only kids, and I expected you to act like adults. That was wrong of me.' He took a sip of his tea. 'It was a bad time all round. Things seemed to collapse about me and I couldn't do anything to stop it. I felt I was losing everything.'

'Jock, don't.' Rebecca consoled him softly.

'And that business with Davie Kelly, Becca,' he went on, 'I wanted to tie you to the island. I saw your restlessness and I thought if you were married and had a couple of kids you'd, well, stay. Didn't work, did it, love?'

'I'm sorry, Jock, I couldn't...' Rebecca shook her head. 'But I'm back now, and I want to help with the farm.'

'How long can you stay?' he asked eagerly. 'I suppose you're on your holidays.'

'Not exactly.' Rebecca pulled a face. 'I've resigned from my job, and so I guess I'm one of the growing ranks of the unemployed.'

Jock frowned in surprise. 'You gave up your job? But I thought you were happy. You got all those promotions.' He smiled at her. 'I was proud of you, love. I mean, I wanted you to come home but, well, I thought you'd made a new life for yourself over there.'

'I thought I had, too,' Rebecca told him. 'But I still felt the pull of home. The island. Bay Ridge. And you and Rudy.' She sighed ruefully. 'We've got two whole years to make up, but you'll see, Jock, now I'm back things will be the same as before. We'll be a family again.'

'Becca——' Jock started and then shook his head again, taking a gulp of his tea.

'And talking about family, how's Rudy? Will he be in for lunch? Is he still grumbling about the bailing?'

Something in Jock's expression silenced Rebecca, and her smile faded.

'Jock, what is it?' she asked. 'Is it Rudy? Is that why you've hired that new foreman? Rudy's not sick, is he?'

'No.' Jock replied at last. 'He's not here.'

'Not here? You mean he left the farm?' Rebecca could scarcely believe it. Although Rudy also continually jibed against Jock, she never imagined he would leave as she had. Somehow she just didn't think Rudy would have had the courage to take such a final step. Rudy was a talker, not a doer; a follower, not a leader. Or so she'd thought.

'Where's he gone?' she asked Jock, and he shrugged.

'I hear he's over in Port Lincoln working on one of the tuna boats.'

Rebecca was speechless. Rudy taking on the demanding job of tuna fishing seemed totally unbelievable.

'You never mentioned in your letters that he'd left.'

Jock made a resigned motion with his hands. 'I didn't want to worry you, Becca.'

'But—when? And why did he leave?' she asked, and Jock sighed again.

'Nearly a year back, and for the same reasons you left,' Jock admitted. 'We argued. We always did. Rudy never would have made a farmer. I knew it but I wouldn't accept that, especially after your father was killed. I wanted him to take over from me when the time came. There've always been Graingers at Bay Ridge, and Rudy was the last.' Jock stopped and ran a hand over his jaw. 'Was I wrong in thinking that way, Becca?' he asked quietly.

Rebecca felt a rush of tears sting her eyes again and she shook her head, scarcely crediting that this could be her grandfather asking for understanding. Jock had never asked for anything in his life. Before he had been like the lighthouse at Cape du Couedic, standing tall, solid and immovable, meeting life head on. Now he was a tired old man.

Pain clutched at Rebecca's heart. She knew she was partially responsible for the change she saw in him.

'We've let you down, haven't we, Rudy and I?' she said brokenly. 'Neither of us gave you a thought. We were too busy thinking about ourselves.'

'No, Becca.' Jock held up his hand. 'No, that's not true. I was the one in the wrong. I tried to dictate your lives. I had no right to do that. I should have known better, but I only wanted to see things from my side. You and Rudy were right to stand up for what you wanted.'

'Oh, Jock, I'm sorry——' Rebecca began.

'Don't be. Your life's for you to live, not me.' Jock patted her shoulder. 'You wouldn't be my flesh and blood if you'd let me take over.' He gave a soft laugh, and Rebecca smiled with him.

She knew what Jock said was true. She was a lot like him in some ways. She could be stubborn too. That was why she had fought with him so much. And it seemed Rudy had had that stubbornness as well.

'With Rudy gone, it's no wonder you needed to put on extra hands,' Rebecca remarked. 'The farm looks great. Have you had a good year?'

'Yes, we've had a good year,' Jock replied.

'That's wonderful.' She beamed across at him.

'Becca.' Jock shifted uncomfortably. 'Becca, things aren't quite like they used to be. Well, things have changed.'

'I can see that. I had a walk around outside. You've expanded. The new shed looks marvellous. You were always talking about pulling down the old one. So you finally got around to it?'

'Not exactly.' Jock stood up and paced across the floor, his hand slowly massaging the small of his back, as though it was aching. He turned back to face her, walking over to lean on the back of his chair.

'When Rudy and I argued before he left last year we were both pretty mad. We said a lot we—well, I—regretted. In anger, I threatened him that I'd sell Bay Ridge

if he went. It didn't stop him going.' Jock's eyes dropped.
'Well, I took a long look at everything. Myself. The farm.
I knew I couldn't possibly keep it going the way things
were, on my own. I'm not young any more, and I'd de-
pended on Rudy's youth more than I realised.' He sighed
heavily. 'So I half decided the only course I could take
was to put Bay Ridge on the market.'

'You mean, sell it? Sell the farm?' Rebecca asked
incredulously.

Jock nodded. 'I tried to go it alone, but by that time
the place had run down. I couldn't keep it up with Rudy
gone, and I couldn't get reliable permanent hands. So I
decided to sell it.'

Rebecca could only stare at him.

'It was the only thing I could do.' Jock shrugged.

'Sell Bay Ridge?' Rebecca repeated softly. 'But you
changed your mind. You didn't sell out after all?' When
her grandfather made no denial Rebecca drew a sharp
breath. 'Jock, you couldn't sell Bay Ridge.' Her voice
broke. 'It's your life.'

Jock looked at her with eyes that were dull and lack-
lustre. 'My life's nearly over,' he said flatly. 'When I
had the offer after Rudy left I took it. It was all I could
do, Becca. I love this place. I couldn't see it run down
around me.'

'But how...? Who...?' A cold shiver of dread
gradually worked its way up her spine, and she found
herself holding her breath, half knowing what Jock was
going to say.

'Who bought Bay Ridge?' Jock raised his eyebrows.
'You met him last night. Byron Willoughby. Will, to his
friends.'

CHAPTER THREE

BYRON WILLOUGHBY. Rebecca cringed inside herself. What had she said to him the night before? She couldn't remember exactly. But she'd treated him as though he was the hired hand. She bit her lip. And Byron Willoughby hadn't set her straight. What right did he have to keep a thing like that from her? He must have had quite a laugh at her expense.

'While Will was at university he spent a vacation here on the island,' Jock was saying, 'and he tells me he never forgot the tranquillity of the place. Actually, Rudy put him on to Bay Ridge. Rudy ran into Will in Port Lincoln and told him I was probably going to put the farm on the market. Will came over to talk to me about it, and he bought me out.'

Rebecca frowned. So Byron Willoughby had lost no time in racing across to take advantage of an old man whose family had deserted him. He'd caught Jock at an extremely vulnerable time and pressed home his advantage. For a buyer looking for a sharp deal, it had been the very best time to negotiate. She felt her lips thin angrily.

'He paid me a fair price,' Jock said, as though he'd read her mind. 'In fact it was more than fair, considering the state of the farm. I had to make a decision and I made it. Will has a feel for the land, Becca, so I knew I was doing the right thing. And when I'm gone, well, the money will see you right, you and Rudy.' Jock's eyes met hers and Rebecca stood up and put her arms around him.

'Oh, Jock, what do I care about money? Bay Ridge is yours to do with as you please.' She felt a lump rise in her throat. Her grandfather was like a fierce old lion that had been tamed.

'I always thought it would be passed on to a Grainger. It was only right. But,' he looked up at her, his eyes dull, 'Rudy didn't have any interest in farming. I knew that years ago. If I'd been honest with myself I'd have admitted it before I alienated him. I tried to make him into another John, but he could never be like his father. I made him feel guilty that he wasn't.' His shoulders sagged wearily. 'I lost your father and then both of you, and now Bay Ridge has passed out of the family.'

'Oh, Jock, I'm sorry,' Rebecca said softly.

Jock nodded. 'I am, too. But things don't turn out the way you want them to just by simply wanting them a particular way. Life's not that easy. It has a habit of turning the tables on us.'

'I wish——' Rebecca stopped. 'And wishing doesn't change the past, either, does it?' she finished, and Jock shook his head.

'But it's not so bad.' He squared his shoulders and drained his teacup. 'Now you're back.' He patted her hand. 'I'm glad you've come home,' he said softly.

Rebecca dropped her head on to his shoulder, overcome that Jock could admit his feelings so freely. Her memories of her grandfather in the years before she'd left had been of a stern, unbending, demanding man. Somehow the radical change in him tore at her heart-strings and filled her with a rush of protective love. They were family and he needed her, had needed her for some time. Perhaps she could coax him back into the grandfather she knew, instead of this tired, disillusioned old man. They could make a home together.

'I'm glad I'm back, too,' she said, and meant it. 'How long will you be staying on the farm? Have you decided where you're going when you leave?'

Jock's face mirrored surprise. 'I'm not leaving, Becca. Will's agreed that I have a home here as long as I like; that was part of the conditions of sale. I was born here on Bay Ridge and I'll die here.'

'That's very generous of him,' Rebecca said thoughtfully.

'Oh, I work for my keep. I'm not completely in my dotage, you know.' His eyes flashed some of their old sparkle. 'Besides, I've worked this farm all my life. I wouldn't know how to stop doing it. Will understood that. He's a good bloke.'

Rebecca looked at him sharply not sure that she hadn't imagined the hastily concealed gleam in her grandfather's eyes.

'What did you think of him?' he asked with apparent casualness.

Rebecca shifted in her chair with an equally casual shrug. 'I arrived pretty late last night, so we didn't really have a chance to talk. And he certainly didn't tell me he was the new owner of Bay Ridge.'

Her gaze went quickly to Jock's face, but his expression was bland. 'He seemed quite nice,' she added and Jock smiled.

Nice. She could almost laugh at that. Nice was far too insipid a word to use when describing Byron Willoughby. Tall. Handsome. Rugged. Downright sexy. Rebecca stopped herself with no little effort and a good deal of shocked surprise. It simply wasn't like her to go on like that about a man. She'd never really been interested enough before.

Apart from Rudy and Jock, who didn't count that way, men hadn't played a very great part in her life. In large numbers they could be fun, but singly they had left her unimpressed. She'd never met a man she admired and respected to the extent that she'd want to spend her whole life with him. Not on the island and not on the mainland.

Growing up hadn't seen her going through any 'boy-crazy' stages. Perhaps she'd had one or two very mild crushes on a couple of pop stars, but no one in her circle of friends had really taken her attention.

And that fiasco with Davie Kelly before she left the island hadn't helped at all. Safety in numbers had been her motto for the past two years.

Then Paul Drewett had put just a small chip in her armour, making her aware of a part of life she'd so far left totally untapped. Did all twenty-two-year-old virgins suddenly feel this way? A sort of restlessness, a yearning for love, to be loved.

And now there was Byron Willoughby. She couldn't deny she found him attractive. Probably *the* most attractive man she'd ever met.

'As I told you, Becca,' Jock was saying, 'Will's a good bloke. Of course, you've heard of him. He's something of a celebrity.'

She forced her attention back to her grandfather. 'Heard of him? Who? Byron Willoughby?' She struggled to pick up the thread of the conversation. 'I thought his name sounded familiar, but I can't place it.'

'In Aussie Rules circles his name's a household word, especially in Victoria. He played for Carlton for years,' Jock told her. 'He played for Port Adelaide originally, but Carlton signed him up and he moved to Victoria. You must have heard of him, love.'

Rebecca's eyes widened, the pieces falling into place in her memory. 'He's *that* Byron Willoughby?' she said incredulously.

Of course. Everyone knew of Willo, as the crowd called him. Rebecca had seen him on TV. He'd been younger then, his hair was shorter, and players on the field looked quite different in ordinary clothes in place of the shorts and the coloured sleeveless jerseys of their football uniforms. She suspected he had come by the small scar on his cheek in one of his games, for Aussie Rules was an exacting body-contact sport.

'That's him.' Jock nodded. 'He made quite a name for himself. He was a fine player, maybe the best. He won the Brownlow Medal a couple of years in a row.'

Once Jock had reminded her, she'd recognised the name in association with the game of Australian Rules Football which was peculiar to Australia. It was extremely fast-moving, supposedly far more demanding of stamina than Rugby League or Rugby Union, and players strove for the utmost speed in every facet of the game. The players, eighteen to a side plus two substitutes, needed to be extremely fit to keep up the gruelling pace for the four twenty-five-minute quarters, and a focal point of the game was the very high leaps of the players to catch or 'mark' the flying ball. The Brownlow Medal was a prestigious award presented each year to the season's best and fairest player.

'I wonder why he gave up the game. I wouldn't have said he was too old,' she reflected. 'And usually a player of his calibre moves into coaching when he retires from actual competition.'

'Said he was disillusioned by it all,' explained Jock, and shook his head. 'And he got his share of bad publicity. A messy business.'

'How was that?' Rebecca couldn't restrain her curiousity.

'Well, he was a hero. The press and the public made him, and all in all they're hard masters to serve. What they make they can break.'

Rebecca gave a half-laugh. 'What did he do to fall from grace?'

'Took a dislike to reporters and photographers. He said he was fed up with their interference in his private life,' replied Jock. 'His and his wife's.'

'Wife?' Rebecca couldn't be sure she actually breathed the word. For a few moments she was completely numb,

and when feeling returned she was hard put to it to ana-
lyse her emotions. Her surprise verged on shock, and
there was something else, something she refused to allow
herself to look at too closely.

She swallowed. 'I didn't realise he was married.'

'She worked on TV, a weather girl. You know, those
pretty young things who come on after the news,' said
Jock. 'Well, that's what she did.'

'Where is she now?' Rebecca was strangely loath to
know the answer, not wanting to picture Byron
Willoughby with an attractive woman by his side.

Jock shook his head sadly. 'She died last year; it was
a car accident, just after Will decided to give up playing
football.'

'How did you discover all this, Jock?' Rebecca asked,
knowing her grandfather's world began and ended on
the island. He'd always treated what happened on the
mainland with irritated indifference.

'I got most of it from Will himself. We often have a
good old chin-wag after dinner. I enjoy it. Usually we
talk about the farm, things like that, but one night he
was a bit down and he told me a little about his life on
the mainland. And, of course, he's also been a bit
worried of late, about young Tammy.' Jock tut-tutted.
'It's all so hard on the kids.'

Rebecca's eyebrows flew upwards. 'He has children?'

'One little girl. She's staying with Will's sister in Port
Lincoln and he gets over to see her when he can. I think
it cuts him up a bit, because the poor little thing wants
to live here on the farm with him. Thinks the world of
her father, does young Tammy. He wanted to have her
here for the school holidays, and as they're coming up
he's been trying to get someone to look after her during
the day.' Jock glanced at Rebecca with a speculative glint
in his eyes. 'He hasn't had much luck to date. Most folks
have enough looking after their own families. Young
Tammy would have been disappointed if she couldn't

come over to the farm—but I've just solved that problem,' he beamed, and paused. 'Now you're here,' he finished with satisfaction.

'Me?' Rebecca queried sharply. 'What exactly do you have in mind, Jock?'

'Well, you could look after Will's little girl,' he said blandly.

'You can't be serious, Jock.' Rebecca laughed. 'I don't know the first thing about children.'

'You don't need to know anything about them. You just trust to instinct.' He smiled at her. 'I think it's a corker idea. And it would sure take a weight from Will's mind.'

'I know I'll have to find a job, but,' she raised her hands and let them fall, 'I was thinking of something clerical.' Rebecca bit gently on her lip. 'If not here on the island, which I know would be practically impossible, then maybe in Adelaide.'

'Why go to the mainland when there's a job right here?' Jock persisted.

'Jock!' Rebecca appealed to him exasperatedly. She was beginning to think she'd been mistaken when she thought her grandfather had changed.

'OK, love.' Jock gave in. 'We'll change the subject. Tell me more about Sydney. What about young men? Did you leave any broken hearts behind you?' Jock winked at her.

'Oh, dozens, Jock,' she teased him back. 'A veritable army of them. There were guys throwing themselves in front of my car as I tried to drive away.'

They laughed together, and Rebecca suddenly felt a finger touch of sensation along her spine. She was unsurprised when she looked around to see a tall, broad body filling the open doorway, and the tingling thrill of anticipation intensified, was joined by a knot of excitement in the pit of her stomach.

Jock's gaze followed Rebecca's and he motioned to the other man to join them. 'Come and have a cuppa, Will. Becca's just brewed a pot. What do you think about my granddaughter coming home?' Jock asked.

'Quite a surprise.' Byron Willoughby replied a little drily.

'It was that. When you told me she was here, Will, I thought my old ears were playing tricks on me. Now here she is, as beautiful as ever.' Jock shook his head. 'It's given me a new lease of life just to see her.'

'I give us twenty-four hours before we come to daggers drawn,' Rebecca teased him, laughing self-consciously.

'I'll admit my granddaughter has a stubborn streak,' Jock laughed too. 'But she wouldn't be a Grainger if she didn't.'

Byron Willoughby's long legs had carried him across the kitchen in a couple of strides, and he pulled his hat off his head, dropping it on to the table as he sat down.

Rebecca's eyes flashed over him before she turned to take a mug from the peg on the dresser and carry it over to the teapot.

In the light of day he was every bit as attractive as she remembered he was. His hat had flattened his dark hair somewhat, but already it was springing back from its confinement. She was immediately aware that she recalled quite vividly the feel of those strands of soft, dark hair as they twined around her fingers, and her hand trembled as she clasped the teapot. A tiny shiver ran the length of her spine and her knees turned shakily to water.

Drawing a steadying breath, she picked up the mug of tea and, her eyes not meeting his, she set it down in front of him. Jock sat smiling, looking from one to the other, and Byron lifted the mug to indicate his thanks. 'Makes a beaut cuppa, does Becca,' beamed Jock.

Byron's attention went back to Jock, and Rebecca realised with surprise that his eyes were in fact blue, and not dark brown or black as she'd surmised they were last night. His eyebrows were straight, dark slashes, and long, black lashes fringed his eyes, accentuating their shape and colour.

Not pretty-boy good-looking like her ex-boss, she decided. No, Byron Willoughby was simply devastatingly handsome. And that small scar was definitely piratical. She laughed inwardly at herself. She couldn't remember ever assessing a man as thoroughly as she had Byron Willoughby, and she couldn't ever remember a man having such an instant and overwhelming effect on her.

She'd always had a built-in defence system keeping anything like that just a safe space away from her. Beginning with Davie Kelly, it had become second nature to her. Even with Paul Drewett her head had governed her actions. But with Byron she suspected her heart could very quickly overrule her head without any trouble at all.

Covertly, Rebecca continued to watch him. His jaw looked even more firm and square, and a faint dark beard-shadow touched his tanned skin. He pursed his lips to sip his tea, and Rebecca's own lips tingled unsettlingly. Last night his mouth had moved over hers, sparking a response that had shaken her with its intensity.

And she was horrified that it could be so, that a man, a stranger, could disarm her so completely. It wasn't a revelation she could rationalise to herself.

She had never been one for idle experimentation. She hadn't looked for that kind of thing. She'd done her share of flirting, especially in those first months after leaving the island, but it had never got out of hand. She'd never allowed it to. Rebecca Grainger was always in command, always called the shots. No one had ever made her feel so out of control. But when Byron Willoughby kissed her, her cool reticence took wing with almost embarrassing swiftness. Frigid? Davie Kelly couldn't have been more mistaken.

At that moment Byron's gaze met hers, held her motionless, drawing her into him until she was sure she saw her own reflection in the deep blue pools of his eyes. She experienced the sensation of drowning, going under, and she tore her eyes from his as she fought for the breath that had lodged in her chest.

'Isn't that right, Becca?' Jock's voice filtered through her stunned immobility.

She blinked, dragging her agitated thoughts together. 'What was that, Jock?' She managed to get her voice to function, if somewhat breathlessly.

'I was saying you could look after young Tammy,' Jock repeated, and Rebecca's eyes flew to Byron Willoughby.

There was a stretched second's silence.

'I'm afraid I have no training or experience in looking after children,' she began hesitantly.

'How long did you intend staying on at Bay Ridge?' Byron asked her, not commenting on what she'd said.

Rebecca felt a rush of irritation to think he had the right to ask her that. But there was no disputing the fact that as the new owner he had every right, and she'd have to apologise to him for her attitude last night. Bay Ridge wasn't her home any more.

She cleared her throat. 'Well, I——'

'She can stay as long as she likes. She gave up her job in Sydney,' Jock put in, and Rebecca cast him a warning glance, unaware that her brown eyes flashed brightly.

'If you're looking for employment, I'm sure we could come to some arrangement,' Byron Willoughby said easily. 'I want my daughter here with me, and it would only be two weeks of full-time babysitting during the school break. That's in a couple of weeks. The rest of the time Tammy would be off to school here on the island.'

Rebecca mulled the idea over in her mind, not wanting to commit herself right on the spot. She felt as though she was being rushed, bulldozed by Jock. Any by Byron Willoughby, even though he was being a little more subtle. But the fact remained that she knew next to nothing about children.

Byron Willoughby stood up and her eyes rose with him. 'Perhaps you could think the idea over and we could discuss it tonight after dinner.'

'Yes. All right.' She glanced back at Jock, who had also climbed to his feet. 'Shall I . . . what time would you like dinner?' she asked.

Jock's face broke into a wide smile and he rubbed his hands together. 'Now that's more like it. I haven't had a decent meal since you left, seems like.' He turned to the other man. 'Becca's a great cook.'

Dark brows rose, and was there a hint of amusement in those deep blue eyes? Rebecca straightened in her chair. Jock was right. She *was* a good cook, and if Byron Willoughby was sceptical then he would find out this evening, her eyes told him.

He gave no sign that he had received the message and made no comment.

'Seven? Seven-thirty?' she challenged.

'Seven would be fine,' he said evenly, turning to walk to the back door. 'Coming Jock?'

'Sure. Won't be a tick.' Jock waited until the younger man had left the kitchen. 'Becca, the job would be just right for you. You wouldn't have to trip over to the mainland, that's if you could manage to find a job in the city. Work's scarce there, I hear. Working for Will would be the best idea, don't you think?'

'But, Jock, I don't know how I'd cope looking after a child,' she appealed to him. 'What if she didn't like me?'

'Don't be ridiculous, Becca,' Jock brushed that aside. 'She's just a little thing, six years old. She'd be no trouble.'

Rebecca grimaced. If one judged young children by some one saw in supermarkets, one couldn't exactly say they were no trouble.

'You think it over, love.' Jock gave her an engaging grin. 'And really make this a slap-up dinner tonight. I'll see you later.' He went to follow Byron Willoughby outside, but turned back before leaving the kitchen. 'It's beaut to have you back, Becca.'

Rebecca stayed sitting at the kitchen table, her hands cradling her now cold cup of tea, and a sudden flood of dismay held her motionless. Surely Jock wasn't matchmaking again? He wouldn't dare. Would he?

In his letters he'd made no mention of selling the farm, even though he'd asked her to come home. Once home, he knew she'd find out about the sale, so why had he...? Had he set the whole scene up? The widowed new owner. A small child in need of a babysitter. An unattached granddaughter. And Bay Ridge.

Rebecca's heartbeats tumbled about in agitation. No, Jock wouldn't have. He couldn't have known how homesick she'd been. Unless he'd read between the lines of her letters. But, even more importantly, he couldn't possibly have imagined there could be anything between herself and Byron Willoughby.

What would an attractive, well-known sportsman, lauded by his fellow players and the public alike, see in the very average Rebecca Grainger, twenty-two, still a virgin and in all probability frigid to boot?

She laughed derisively at herself, but stopped when she realised she had laughed aloud and that the sound was just slightly high and shaky and held a note of anticipatory excitement.

No, she told herself firmly. She wasn't going to be hounded by her grandfather or anyone else. She wasn't going to be pressured into taking on this job or... or Byron Willoughby. Her lips twisted wryly. Perhaps she should revise her first impression of Jock. It seemed that he hadn't changed all that much. Not deep down. Here he was, manipulating her life again, and she'd only just arrived.

Admittedly he was using far more acceptable tactics than he had in the past—no loud, booming voice bent on domination. Now it was softer, although still as single-minded, pulling on her emotions. The crafty old devil! she smiled reluctantly to herself.

But what should she do? If she didn't take this job, it would mean moving out of Bay Ridge. Now that the farm no longer belonged to her grandfather she couldn't possibly intrude on Byron Willoughby's hospitality. She looked around the familiar kitchen and sighed sadly. Nothing stayed the same. She'd been more than a little foolish to think it would have.

Rebecca frowned thoughtfully. If she decided to accept the position, she'd have to stay in close proximity to Byron Willoughby. Did she want that? Could she handle it? was really what she meant. Of course she could, she assured herself irritably. She was a grown woman, and if he was an attractive man, so what? There were plenty around.

Not quite like Byron Willoughby, the thought jeered from deep inside her. And not a man who had the effect on her that he had. Yet why should that surprise her? He probably evoked the same reaction from all the women he met. He wasn't exactly a callow youth. Moving in the circles he had in Melbourne as a star football player, he would have been able to pick and choose from a stream of females. If she remembered rightly, she'd seen a spread on him in a popular woman's magazine— the usual thing, scenes of some of his triumphs, his highest 'marks', kicking a goal, drinking champagne from a huge silver cup, bikini-clad lovelies all around him.

How she disliked that type of man. She'd probably find he had an ego to match his fantastic physique.

But none of this brought her any nearer to resolving her problems. To stay on at Bay Ridge or return to the mainland? She stood up and went through to her bedroom, absently finishing her unpacking. Only when she'd stowed the last of her books on the bookshelves did it cross her mind that she needn't have completely unpacked if she was leaving.

Leaving. Her lips twisted in a wry smile. She didn't think she had ever had any intention of leaving, not even when she discovered that Jock had sold Bay Ridge. She wanted to stay. She wanted to make those two years up to Jock. He was an old man and he needed her. Byron Willoughby's kiss had nothing whatsoever to do with any decision she made. She impressed this on herself very forcefully.

She spent some time taking stock of the food situation, but eventually she found all the ingredients for Jock's favourite meal—roast beef and baked vegetables. The freezer was well stocked with meat, and there were vegetables and plenty of canned foodstuffs arranged tidily in the larder.

When everything was under control, she slipped along to the bathroom for a shower and was back in her bedroom brushing her dark hair when she heard footsteps pass her room. Jock and Byron Willoughby were back.

She looked down at her plain light grey skirt and pale pink blouse, and wondered if she should have simply stayed in her slacks and sweater. They never used to dress for dinner at Bay Ridge, but now—— She ran her fingers over the front of her blouse. It had long, full sleeves caught into wide cuffs at the wrist, and she knew the pale pastel shade suited her dark colouring.

Suit her or not, she was being foolish again, and exasperatedly she picked up a matching grey waistcoat and slipped it on. She had almost finished setting the table

when Byron Willoughby joined her, and the sight of him
held her fingers motionless.

His dark hair was still damp from his shower, the ends
having a tendency to curl, and he had obviously just
shaved, his jaw smooth and clean. He smelled of a tangy
shaving cream, and Rebecca had an almost over-
powering urge to run her fingers along the contours of
his cheek and jaw. A pale blue knitted shirt moulded his
muscular shoulders, and his dark blue trousers hugged
his narrow hips and the long length of his legs.

Rebecca was completely breathless, and had to force
herself to look away from him and continue setting out
the cutlery. She dropped a fork with a nervous clatter.

'Would you care for something to drink?' he asked,
and the sound of his voice, although she was half
expecting him to speak, made her start. Her nerve-
endings vibrated in response to his deep, resonant tone.

'No, thank you. I don't think so. I don't drink much,'
she heard herself stammer, knowing her own voice
sounded forced and unnatural. If she tried to swallow
anything just at the moment she was sure she'd choke.

She couldn't, dared not allow herself to look at him
again, but her body was tantalisingly attuned to his
movements. She felt him cross to the sideboard, heard
the clink of ice in a glass, the splash of liquid. And then
he was standing by the table, only inches from her.

'Can I help?' he asked with seeming ease.

'No thanks. I've finished now.' She stole a sideways
glance at him and found her eyes caught on him as he
raised his glass to his lips. He took a mouthful of amber
liquid, swallowed, the strong muscles of his neck con-
tracting, mesmerising her.

The air between them thickened, sparked an awareness
that held Rebecca helpless. Was he conscious of it, too?
He had to be. She could feel herself being pulled towards
him. If she didn't say something, she was terribly afraid
she was going to make a complete and utter fool of

herself. She drew herself together with faltering will-power.

'Dinner's ready. Will Jock be long?' She glanced towards the hallway leading to the back bedroom. She couldn't hear him moving about. 'Maybe I should go and hurry him along.'

Byron Willoughby watched her from beneath his half-closed lids but, before he could comment, the outer kitchen door opened and Jock strode through into the dining-room.

He ran a hand over his windswept white hair. 'Ah!' He let out an exclamation of pleasure as he took in the placemats and cutlery and the bowl of flowers in the centre of the table. 'Just like old times. Sure beats eating at the kitchen table, doesn't it, Will?' He smiled broadly and lifted his head. 'And smells fit for a king, too.'

'It does that,' Byron agreed blandly.

'If you'll both sit down, I'll serve it up.' Rebecca left them.

In the kitchen she took a few seconds to gather herself together. This would never do, she told herself irritatedly, and she walked resolutely towards the stove.

Surprisingly, the meal passed quite easily, and Rebecca actually managed to do some justice to her food. The two men discussed the farm, in much the same way that Jock had talked with Rudy all those years ago, in the odd moments when they weren't arguing. Occasionally Jock would stop to bring Rebecca up to date with the various improvements Byron had made about the place.

'You'll have to come out one day and see what Will's done,' Jock told her enthusiastically. 'I reckon we'll nearly double the yield with this year's crops, and now we're gradually clearing the whole of the west paddock.'

'I thought you were going to leave that part of the farm because you were worried about it being too close to the salt-liable areas,' Rebecca remarked to Jock.

She knew her grandfather had always wanted to work that paddock but, apart from never having the time or the men to do it, he had been wary of increasing the chance of the occurrence of salinity by clearing the scrub. Salinity in the soil was a prevalent problem with which Kangaroo Island farmers had to cope.

'Will's gone into all that,' Jock told her. 'We're going to try some different types of drainage and chisel-ploughing, and we'll be experimenting with seeding to salt-tolerant plants.'

'I see.' So Byron Willoughby had it all worked out.

For herself, she had loved the untouched wilderness of that part of the farm, the waist-high grasses, the thick groves of the many-trunked king mallee trees, clustered splashes of green, gold and rust, right down to the more barren looking vegetation of the less arable land. Now it was being cleared, to be wild no more.

She looked across at Byron Willoughby, to find his eyes on her, and she had the distinct feeling that he could see into her mind.

'I'd like to apologise,' Rebecca swallowed. 'For last night,' she finished quickly, and Byron raised one dark brow enquiringly. 'I was unaware that Jock had sold the farm. I thought you just worked here,' she explained, feeling herself flush with an embarrassed resentment.

Jock chuckled. 'Put you nicely in your place, too, I'll bet, Will. That's her grandmother in her.'

Byron smiled and shrugged easily.

'You didn't enlighten me,' she said, flashing Jock a censorious look, and unable to keep the note of rebuke from her tone.

'You'd had a long day. And it was late.' Byron folded his table napkin and sat back in his chair. 'I thought explanations could wait.'

How she wished he wasn't so solicitious. And so self-assured. The glow of amusement in his eyes only raised her ire. She sat up stiffly and took a steadying breath.

There was no point in starting an argument with him, not here in front of Jock.

'How many hands do you have working on Bay Ridge now?' she asked evenly, carefully setting down her dessert-spoon.

'Four, with Jock.' Byron smiled at the older man.

'You'd remember the Macklin boys, Greg and Doug?' Jock asked, and Rebecca nodded. 'Then there's young Mike, the youngest of the O'Learys from down the road. And, of course, there's me.' Jock drained the last mouthful of his beer. 'It sure makes a difference having enough men to keep the place in shape. Will's the best thing to happen to Bay Ridge in years.'

Rebecca slid a glance to Byron. His eyes met hers and she caught the edge of an amused mockery in their dark blue depths.

'Jock tells me you played Australian Rules Football professionally,' she said, nettled by the expression on his face.

'For a few years, yes.'

'So Carlton's loss was Bay Ridge's gain?' she quipped with a cool smile. 'You must find the life here on Kangaroo Island quite a comedown after the whirlwind of Melbourne.'

Byron shrugged. 'Not really. Having experienced both life-styles as you have, you'd have to agree that Bay Ridge has a lot going for it,' he challenged, his words finding the vulnerable place inside her that had sent her seeking home and the peace and leisurely pace of the island.

But he couldn't know that. Or could he? How much about her had Jock told him? Her eyes sought his again, but she could glean nothing from his expression.

'That it has,' put in Jock. 'Don't you think so, Becca?'

'Of course. You know I've always loved the farm and the island.' She turned back to Byron. 'I believe you visited the island some years ago?'

'Not that many years ago.' His lips lifted in a crooked grin that made his blue eyes twinkle, and Rebecca felt her breath catch somewhere in her chest. He really was attractive...

'I studied agricultural science at university,' Byron was saying, and her eyes were caught on the shape, the upward curve of his lips as he spoke. 'We came over to Kangaroo Island on a field trip one term. I guess it wove a spell around me then, and the chance to live here wasn't one I could pass up.'

'But don't you regret giving up your football career?' Rebecca asked.

'No.'

Rebecca sat back in her chair. 'Not even the roar of the crowds? What sort of attendances do they get at the grand finals? Over a hundred thousand? All chanting your name?'

Byron shook his head.

'Or the girls? The fans who flock around you as they do around pop stars? Don't you miss them?' Rebecca smiled sweetly, knowing she was being a little bitchy, but unable to stop herself.

'Now, how shall I answer that, Becca?' he asked softly. 'If I say I do miss them you'll say "Ah ha! I knew it." If I deny it, you'll smile at me in disbelief.' He laughed, and she sensed a touch of bitterness. 'The media paints a glossy picture, but believe me, to keep at the top and justify my place on the team I had to work hard. Wine, women and song don't mix very well with hard training, not if you're serious about the game.'

And to have been so applauded by the public and his fellow players Byron Willoughby must have been serious about the game, Rebecca realised.

'What made you give it up?' she asked. 'I think I read somewhere that you had a knee operation. Was that it?'

His lashes fell, effectively shuttering the expression in his eyes. 'Partly.' He shrugged. 'I felt the time had come to make the break.'

'Just thinking about running over a football oval for nearly two hours makes me feel very tired.' Jock yawned. 'That was a bonzer meal, love. Sure makes my baked beans on toast down at the cottage very unappetising.'

Rebecca turned to look at Jock. 'Down at what cottage?'

'The old cottage, the first family homestead on Bay Ridge,' Jock replied. 'I've moved in down there.'

CHAPTER FOUR

'You're living down at the old cottage?' Rebecca's voice was thin and high, mirroring her incredulity.

'Yes.' Jock smiled. 'And I've got it all set up lovely. I took my old chair with me and a few of my bits and pieces.'

'But I thought——' Rebecca darted a glance at Byron and back to her grandfather. 'I didn't know you——' she stammered.

'Well, I felt more at home there than I did rattling around this house after you and Rudy left, so I shut the house up and moved down to the cottage. This place is too big for a man alone. Don't you think, Will?' he addressed Byron. 'It needs a family. It will do the old place good to have young people around it again. Absolutely ideal place to raise kids. Why, young Tammy loved it when she was here before.'

Byron was absently rubbing his jaw with his hand. 'She did that,' he acquiesced softly, and Rebecca sensed the worry behind the slight frown on his brow. 'Tammy spent her last school break here,' he told Rebecca. 'I had a young girl come out from Kingscote to look after her, but she's married now and expecting a baby of her own. So,' he shrugged, 'if I can't find a replacement, I guess Tammy will have to stay in Port Lincoln with my sister.'

'Tsk! A pity!' Jock shook his white head. 'A farm's the best place for a youngster to grow up.'

Rebecca gave Jock a restraining look that went completely over his head.

'Thought any more about taking the job on, Becca?' he asked blandly.

'Not exactly,' she replied cautiously. 'I'm not quite sure what the position entails.'

'Oh, it would be a piece of cake. You just keep an eye on young Tammy, cook us some more meals like this one and there you are.' Jock raised his hands, beaming as though she couldn't ask for more out of life. Her grandfather was still a male chauvinist of the finest order.

'Perhaps it might be better if I did the explaining about the job and all it involves, Jock,' Byron remarked drily.

'Sure, Will.' Jock nodded, not daunted in the least. 'It will do my old heart good to see a family back in the homestead.' He sighed reminiscently. 'When Becca's grandmother and I moved in here, we hoped we'd have a whole parcel of kids.' He took out his pipe. 'But we only had John, Becca's father. We lost two babies at birth, and after that Becca's grandmother was a little poorly. I lost her when she was barely thirty-five. When John gave me two grandchildren I couldn't have been happier. My Becca——' he motioned his pipe at Rebecca, '——Becca here was named for her grandmother—well, my Becca would have been thrilled too. Now I'm waiting for some great-grandchildren, and I won't deny I thought I'd have some by now.'

Rebecca felt a flood of colour wash her cheeks, and she stood up. 'I think I'll clear the table. Anyone for another helping of dessert?'

The two men declined.

'We'll help with the dishes.' Byron began to stack their plates.

'No, please. You and Jock finish your coffee. It won't take me long to put these into the dishwasher,' she hastened to assure them, and disappeared into the kitchen with her pile of plates.

She was pleased to make her escape before her grandfather's comments grew more personal. She could hear the two men talking about the west paddock, and eventually she had everything tidied away, leaving her no reason not to rejoin them. Jock was pushing himself slowly to his feet.

'Well, it's past my bedtime. I'll leave you two to talk over the job in question. See you tomorrow, Will.' He patted Rebecca's arm as she kissed his weathered cheek. 'Thanks for the nice meal, love, I enjoyed it. And having you back at Bay Ridge has made your old grandfather very happy. Families shouldn't separate the way ours did. But now you're home where you belong.'

Rebecca couldn't meet Byron's eyes.

Jock walked through the kitchen and opened the back door. Taking the torch he'd left on the cupboard, he gave them one final smile that enveloped the two of them, and then stepped out into the night to disappear into the darkness.

Oh, no! A cold shiver skittered down the length of Rebecca's spine. Why hadn't she called him back? Jock's living down at the cottage meant she was here all alone in the house with Byron Willoughby. The full import of the situation became startlingly clear to her with her grandfather's departure.

How could Jock just walk away and leave her? Surely he must realise it wasn't right that she should be sharing the house with a man. A very attractive man. Alone. Jock was old-fashioned when it came to the proprieties. And yet he had gone down to the old homestead, leaving them together.

She recalled his knowing parting smile. Good grief, he was matchmaking! What would Byron Willoughby be thinking? For he must have seen that transparent look on Jock's face too, and known what it meant. Rebecca felt herself flushing again.

'Look, Mr Willoughby,' she began, 'about this job.' There was no way she could stay under these circumstances.

'Call me Byron, or Will, if you prefer,' he said and gave her a crooked smile. 'Mr Willoughby still sounds more suited to my father.'

That smile completely disarmed Rebecca, and the tight ball of her aggression dissolved and melted away. She had to develop some defence against him, she told herself. He was positively lethal.

'Come on through to the living-room. We might as well discuss the job in comfort.'

He motioned for her to precede him, and she led the way along the hall to the front of the house. Soon they were seated on either side of the fireplace, facing each other, as they had been the evening before. After he'd kissed her. Rebecca's hands tightened where they were clasped together in her lap. She mustn't think about that kiss. She mustn't allow it to colour her decision about staying or leaving.

'The job will involve supervising my daughter,' Byron was saying, 'and although I want you to take the position I feel it's only fair to tell you that looking after a lively six-year-old isn't exactly a sinecure.' He grimaced. 'Especially with my six-year-old daughter. I love her, but I have to admit there are times when she can be a bit of a handful, like most kids. That's one of the reasons I want her here with me. My sister needs a break. Laurel has two children of her own, and I can't help feeling I'm taking advantage of her by leaving Tammy with her for so long. On top of that my young brother has been staying with them too, until our parents arrive home in a few weeks from a trip abroad.'

'How long has Tammy been living with your sister?' Rebecca asked.

'For almost a year. Before that we lived in Melbourne and I had her with me. But since I took over the farm I've had to be out all day and, much as I wanted to, there was no way I could have her here.'

He frowned slightly. 'She's only six years old and we've been separated for too long. I don't want her growing away from me.'

Standing up, he paced across the floor, stopping with his back to her, one hand massaging the muscles in the back of his neck. 'She's my responsibility, apart from anything else. And God knows, she needs a better break than she's had up till now,' he added softly, his voice so low Rebecca had to strain to catch it.

She felt a stirring of compassion for the child, little more than a baby, losing her mother and then having to be separated from her father. Rebecca's own mother had died when she was barely a year old, so the only memories she had of her came from a few old photographs. But, growing up, she'd still had her father, her brother and Jock. She could imagine how traumatic it all must have been for Tammy.

Byron Willoughby turned back to face her and walked over to sit on the arm of his chair.

'I can understand that Tammy would want to be with you,' she said gently. 'I mean, losing her mother and——'

Her voice died away at the expression on Byron's face. Or perhaps the lack of expression would have been a far more accurate description. It was as though a shutter fell over his features, a blank mask that concealed his feelings, and she thought she saw a nerve flicker in the controlled set of his jaw. He stood up and resumed his stance some distance from her.

Obviously the mention of his wife was still painful for him. And the revelation drew an answering pain in Rebecca, for far different reasons. 'Jock said your wife was killed in a car accident.' Rebecca watched his closed face for a flicker of emotion, but there was none. He was giving nothing away.

'Yes. Tammy was a little too young to understand it all at the time.' His lips thinned, and the expression Rebecca was looking for appeared for brief seconds.

But where she'd expected pain she saw only a bitter anger, and his hands were clenched into tight fists. Why was he so angry? Was he railing against fate for depriving Tammy of her mother, for taking his wife from him? He must have loved her very much. She swallowed achingly, wanting to reach out to him.

'How long would the job be likely to last?' she asked, changing the subject.

Byron sighed, his hands going to rest momentarily on his hips before he crossed to sit down in his chair again. He was restless, almost nervous, Rebecca would have said. But he couldn't be! Not a man as self-possessed as this one so obviously was. His hands rested along the arms of the chair, his fingers quietly drumming on the soft leather.

'I want Tammy to make this her home, too, so the job would be an indefinite one.' He gave a crooked smile that didn't reach his eyes. 'But if you're not looking for a permanent position, perhaps you would consider staying until I could find someone suitable.'

'Well,' Rebecca hovered on the brink of accepting, while part of her cried out for her to put as much space between herself and Byron Willoughby as she could manage, 'I suppose I could do it to help out until you find someone else. I mean, I'm here now, so I may as well make myself useful.' She gave him a faint smile.

'Fine.' He seemed to relax, the tension leaving the firm line of his jaw. 'I really appreciate it. So,' he smiled back at her, turning her stomach to quivering jelly, 'we should talk about wages.'

Rebecca's eyes flew to meet his. 'Oh, no. Really, I would rather just help out.' She bit her lip. 'Now that I've found out that Bay Ridge no longer belongs to Jock, I couldn't possibly presume to stay here as though he still owns the place. I mean, I could look after Tammy and do the cooking for my keep.'

Byron's brows drew together in a frowning line. 'That's ridiculous. You'll be doing a fair job, so you deserve, and you'll get, a fair wage.' He mentioned an amount that had Rebecca's mouth gaping.

'But——'

'No buts, Becca. I insist.'

His smooth, deep voice saying her name took all resistance out of her, his tone washing over her with nerve-honing awareness, and the memory of their embrace the night before flooded back to her. She felt his eyes move over her, knew by the responsive tingle of each nerve-ending that he was remembering, too.

On the heels of their heightened consciousness of each other came the recollection that they were alone together in the house, and if he wanted to kiss her again—— The worst part about it was the knowledge that she would be powerless to prevent him, that she wouldn't want to stop him.

'When were you thinking of bringing Tammy home?' she asked, striving to restore their conversation to a more casual level.

'It's not quite the end of term, so I suppose it would be best to leave her with Laurel until the school break in two weeks' time,' he replied easily. 'Then she can begin the next term here on the island.'

Two weeks. Rebecca bit her lip and swallowed painfully. She couldn't stay here alone with him for so long.

'I see. I think perhaps it might be better if I moved into Kingscote until, well, just until Tammy comes over from Port Lincoln. I...' Her voice died away.

His lashes shielded the expression in his eyes, but the same nerve beat a pulse in his jaw. 'Why?' he asked flatly.

'Because,' Rebecca swallowed again, 'I thought, perhaps it might be better...' her voice faded away again.

'You said that before,' he remarked drily. 'I presume you're referring to our isolation here in the house.'

'Well, yes.' Rebecca lifted her chin. 'I think I should move into town. Or maybe Jock could come back to the house.'

His eyes watched her, a faint hint of mockery in their depths, in the twist of his lips. 'Does all this maidenly timidity have something to do with last night?' He raised one dark eyebrow coldly.

Rebecca's fingers twisted agitatedly together in her lap. 'Of course not. It's just that the island's close-knit and,' she paused and swallowed, 'people talk.'

'Perhaps I should apologise, should I, Becca?' he asked quietly, as though she hadn't spoken.

'Oh, no!' Rebecca's face flamed. 'I didn't expect . . . it was a simple misunderstanding.'

'A misunderstanding? Yes, you thought I was your brother.'

'Well, yes,' she told him.

His eyebrow went up again. 'Do you always kiss your brother so——' he paused '—thoroughly?'

'No, of course not,' Rebecca assured him forcefully, anger stirring in her at his insinuation. 'When I . . . when I kissed you, I knew you weren't Rudy.'

He smiled, but she sensed he wasn't amused. 'I'm pleased about that.' His tone dripped biting sarcasm and Rebecca stood up angrily.

'Look, it was a mistake. I'd appreciate it if you would simply forget it ever happened,' she threw at him.

'Forget it happened?' he repeated quietly.

'Yes.'

'Can you forget it, Becca?' he asked, and the air about them stilled, that same tension rising to engulf them.

'Yes, I can,' she cried, and didn't even believe it herself.

Byron made no comment, but just sat watching her, and she felt his eyes probing down into her very soul.

'Last night I was tired. I'd been travelling for days. It was my first time home in two years. Maybe my emotions were close to the surface because of all that.'

He lifted his hand, one long finger absently rubbing his cheek. 'Meaning any reasonably acceptable male would have been awarded the same attention?' he queried.

'Yes. No.' Rebecca shook her head and had to fight down the urge to stamp her foot. 'Oh, I don't know!' she finished exasperatedly.

His cynical smile incensed her further. How could she ever have thought he was handsome? He was a big-headed, sarcastic, infuriating...

'And anyway,' she challenged him, 'I don't recall you fending me off with cries of "Oh, horror!"'

His grin broadened, driving deep creases down his cheeks, bracketing his mouth, his blue eyes crinkling at the corners. Rebecca blinked defensively. Genuine amusement made him, impossibly, even more devastatingly attractive.

'I didn't, did I? But then what red-blooded male in his right mind would refuse such an enjoyable experience?'

Rebecca's chin lifted and her brown eyes sparkled with an anger she was having trouble sustaining. She searched vainly for something scathing to retort, but all thought of a suitable rejoinder left her as he stood up and closed the space between them, his hand reaching out to clasp her arm. His touch seared through the thin material of her blouse.

'Look, Becca, I apologise. How's that? I thought you were a girlfriend of Rudy's. If I'd known you were his sister and Jock's granddaughter—well,' he shrugged, 'it wouldn't have happened.' His lips moved upwards in that shattering smile. 'At least, I don't think it would have.'

Rebecca's eyes were locked on his lips. This close, she could see their distinct outline, almost feel their cool firmness moving so evocatively on her own. He could bend her so easily, mould her, have her at his mercy. Did he know that? She mustn't allow him to——

'Please take your hand off me,' she said with steely control, and his eyes fell to where his fingers clasped her arm, tightening.

Then his gaze rose again to lock with hers, anger deepening their blueness to black. A tremor of fear clutched at her stomach, but as she held his gaze she saw the subtle change in his expression as his anger was augmented by a far more potent emotion.

Her body surged immediately to life, her response to that message in his eyes overriding her own anger, and her heartbeats thundered loudly in her ears.

They stood motionless, his hard fingers still folded around her arm, their bodies crying out for contact, for each other's touch, and the air between them seemed to glow and spark with the intensity of their mutual awareness.

From some way very far off Rebecca realised she was losing control again. She shouldn't, couldn't let it happen. Could she? She knew without a shred of doubt that if he put his lips to hers she'd be totally and irrevocably lost. She'd be putty in his hands, his to lead who knew where.

Where? She jeered at herself. Where else? If he wanted to carry her across the hall to his bed, she had a terrified, ebullient feeling that she would let him. And then where would all her principles be, the moral values she'd professed so adamantly that she intended to keep?

She couldn't allow the situation to go that far. She couldn't let him get that close to her. He was to be her employer, just as Paul Drewett had been. So where was the difference? Wasn't this the situation she'd left in Sydney repeating itself?

Rebecca shook her head, her eyes burning brightly as she looked up into his, fighting to blot out the answering flame that glowed just as brilliantly in their dark depths.

'No,' she breathed. 'Please, Byron. Don't.'

He shifted his weight and she held out her hands to ward him off.

'No,' she repeated, a little more firmly this time.

'Becca,' he breathed her name huskily, the sound in itself a soft, erosive caress.

'No!' She took a few faltering steps backwards towards the door, away from him, away from the potent persuasiveness of the feel of him, the touch of him, the musky male fragrance of him.

He came towards her and she backed further away.

'No. I don't want you to touch me.' She shook her head. 'And I'm beginning to believe that being pawed by one's employer is mandatory for women.'

He lifted his head, his expression closing, hardening. 'What exactly is that supposed to mean?'

'I would have said it was self-explanatory.'

'Not to me.'

Rebecca shrugged, outwardly aloof while inside she quivered with a disconcerting combination of arousal and apprehension. 'My boss in Sydney also made it quite clear that other services were expected from me besides my secretarial skills.'

'I see.' His lips tightened in to a thin, angry line. 'And these other services, surely they earned you a bonus?' One dark eyebrow quirked sarcastically.

'No, of course they didn't, because the services were assuredly not rendered.' Rebecca felt a flush wash over her face. 'Why do you think I resigned from what was a very good position and a job I liked?'

'I think you've made your point, Miss Grainger,' he remarked icily. 'But let me clarify mine. I'm not so desperate to get a woman into my bed that I have to pay one to be there. This job is purely and simply to look after my daughter's needs. Most definitely not mine. I'm quite capable of looking after my own——' he paused for just a split second '—wants. I hope I'm making myself clear. I'm also not in the habit of taking advantage of employees. However, as you seem to think I am and it's happened before, then perhaps you'd be advised to look to yourself for possible causes. Maybe you're not giving off the right, shall we say, vibes.'

'Are you implying——?' Rebecca spluttered angrily.

'An essay in contradiction? Yes meaning no, do you think?'

'Why, you arrogant, self-opinionated, egotistical——'

'Last night your response was somewhat exuberant, you can't deny that.' He raised his hands and let them fall. 'What's my ego got to do with that? You should be thanking me from the bottom of your maidenly heart for not taking advantage of what was so willingly offered.'

'You're exaggerating.' Rebecca got out through angrily clenched teeth, and he laughed quietly.

'I don't think I am. So,' Byron shoved his hands in to the pockets of his trousers, 'now that we understand each other, if you feel I misunderstood your particular vibes,' he inclined his head sardonically, 'then I apologise.' There was no remorse in his tone. 'I'll be sure I see it doesn't happen again.'

Their eyes held, warred, dark brown anger burning into cold blue self-possession.

'The job, minus any strings, is yours if you want it, Miss Grainger,' he added after long moments.

And what did he expect her to say to that? Rebecca asked herself for the umpteenth time that week. In the cold light of day their exchange had seemed just a little unreal, as though it had happened to someone else and not her.

And not to a man like Byron Willoughby, for heaven's sake!

For all his clipped protestations, she had a feeling Byron wasn't as unmoved by her rejection of him as he professed to be. He could hardly be used to women turning down his advances.

Rebecca grimaced. Fortunately, he couldn't know what it had cost her to deny herself the heady pleasure of his touch, the caresses she'd sampled so devastatingly that first night.

And, lying in bed afterwards, her body had ached with an unfamiliar yearning. If she hadn't stopped him he would have made love to her. How she'd wished he had. And even now...

Rebecca flushed at her thoughts. What was wrong with her? She was behaving like a frustrated old maid, much as she detested that description. What was that elusive quality that made Byron Willoughby so different from the men she'd known in the past? For he *was* different. He had been from the moment they'd met.

In the accepted sense of the word she'd seen men who were far more handsome than Byron was, but, when he'd kissed her, her reaction had been so radically new to her that she'd simply melted into him.

Yet, after all he'd said, his insinuations about her leading him on, she'd accepted the position he'd offered. She tried to tell herself it was because she had no other job to go to, that she wanted to stay on Bay Ridge with Jock. But, as much as she refused to face the fact, she sensed deep down her decision had more to do with Byron Willoughby than she could admit to herself.

There was an awareness, a spark of electricity, a smouldering ember between them that repelled and enticed at the same time. And sharing the house with him was only adding to the volatile atmosphere that she couldn't deny existed between them.

At least there had been little opportunity for them to be alone together. Byron had always left the house by the time Rebecca rose, and Jock came up to the house to share the evening meal with them. It was relatively easy to slip off to her room as Jock left. But one thing was certain, she told herself, she shouldn't be taking on this job of looking after his daughter. Their awareness of each other simmered too close to the surface for comfort. If she was sensible, Rebecca grimaced wryly, she'd drive right back on to the *Troubridge* and escape from the island. And from Byron Willoughby.

But she was committed now. Byron had telephoned his sister in Port Lincoln the morning after Rebecca had agreed to look after his little girl, telling her he would be collecting Tammy at the end of the school term, so the die had been cast. Byron's sister would have told Tammy she would be coming home, and Rebecca couldn't bring herself to disappoint the child.

She sighed. Now look what you've got yourself into, she chastised herself as she drove back to Bay Ridge from Kingscote township. She stopped at the post-box to collect the mail as she turned in through the gates leading up to the house.

Her trip into Kingscote had made her a little late in preparing their dinner. Byron came in and showered and then, to her consternation, sat himself down at the kitchen table to read his mail while she put the finishing touches to their meal. To have him sitting there threw all her hard-won composure out the window. Since their emotion-charged conversation the day after her arrival, he had dropped an invisible wall down between them. At least, that was what it had felt like to Rebecca. He spoke to her when he had to, looked at her, but his face seemed devoid of any expression.

And, perversely, she wanted the warmth back, the glow that grew between them and set her heartbeats fluttering. What was happening to her? She was a mass of contradictions, swinging first one way and then the other.

She slid a glance across at Byron. He was reading one of his letters, a hand-written one, and judging by the frown creasing his brow whatever the letter contained was not giving him very pleasant news. One long finger rubbed his chin reflectively and he threw the letter on to the table, continuing to gaze at it broodingly.

'Damn,' he muttered softly, and then looked up to find Rebecca watching him.

'Bad news?' she asked evenly, trying to take a page out of his book by keeping the atmosphere between them casually businesslike.

'Not exactly.' He pushed himself to his feet and somewhat absently carried the cutlery through to the dining-room, to return a moment later. 'It was from my mother,' he told her. 'The letter.'

Rebecca's eyebrows rose in surprise, and a crooked smile momentarily lit his face.

'I do have a mother. And a father,' he remarked wryly. 'Don't you believe me?'

'If you say so,' she smiled back. 'In fact, I believe you mentioned them the other day. They're overseas, aren't they?'

He nodded, some of his previous tension leaving him, and his tall body relaxed as he leant one hip against the cupboard and folded his arms.

'In London at present. They left three months ago and we expected them back next week.' He frowned slightly again. 'They're enjoying it so much they've decided to stay on. Dad's retired, so there's no reason for them to hurry back.'

'It sounds like they must be having a great time,' Rebecca commented, wondering how this posed a problem.

'Mmm. They planned the trip for years.' He rubbed the line of his jaw with his hand. 'Mum's worried about my young brother,' he explained. 'She didn't want to leave him at home unsupervised, so he's been staying with Laurel and Bill.'

'How old is he?'

'Seventeen.' Byron grimaced. 'And going through a very trying stage, to quote my mother. He matriculated with honours last year but can't seem to decide what he wants to do with his life, apart from moping around making a complete nuisance of himself, worrying our parents to death.'

'Aren't you being a little hard on him?' suggested Rebecca. 'When you're seventeen, it's difficult to try to make a decision that will ultimately affect the whole of your life.'

Byron gave a short laugh. 'You sound like Mum. She's forever making excuses for him. But as far as I'm concerned Dad should have kicked Kym in the backside and told him to get into line ages ago. Beneath all his angry-young-man histrionics he has a good brain. He's just too lazy to use it.'

'And did your father have to kick you in the backside too?' Rebecca asked casually, trying to keep a straight face.

'No, he didn't.' Byron glared at her.

'So you did everything that was expected of you?'

He gazed at her through narrowed eyes, and he must have caught the hint of a suppressed smile on her lips for he straightened, his hands resting on his hips.

'Something tells me I'm being got at,' he said coolly, and expelled an expressive breath. 'OK, so I had my fling, too, but I knew I had to get some kind of qualifications for after the party was over.'

'And your brother probably realises that as well.' Rebecca shrugged. 'I think your father's right in giving him a little time to decide what he wants to do.'

'Oh, you do?' Byron was glaring again.

'And besides, I'm nearer to your brother's age,' she teased. 'I don't have as far back to remember what seventeen was like as you do.'

A chuckle bubbled up inside Rebecca at the stunned look on his face, but he recovered quickly and took a couple of paces towards her. Rebecca kept the table between them.

'That crack was below the belt,' he said menacingly. 'I'm not exactly bordering on senility.'

'I didn't say you were.' Rebecca stepped hastily out of his reach.

'Not in so many words.' Byron lunged and with little effort caught her arm, bringing her up against his taut body. 'Now. You were saying?' His eyes gleamed with amusement as Rebecca tried unsuccessfully to twist out of his hold.

'I was just joking, of course,' she assured him. 'You don't look a day older than twenty-five.'

His eyebrows rose. 'Twenty-five? Your worst fault, Miss Grainger, is over-acting,' he added wryly as a chuckle escaped from Rebecca's lips, more the result of her nervousness than amusement. 'I'm thirty-three, if you must know. Does that make me past it?'

'Past what?' Her nerve-endings were clamouring as a growing knot of that same tension rose so easily to the surface.

Byron grimaced. 'Past pawing you, I guess,' he said softly, mockingly holding her gaze.

Rebecca's lips quivered and his eyes fell to dwell on them, making her suddenly light-headed, as though he had physically traced their outline. Her heartbeats thudded, rising to almost choke her.

'I'm... I suppose I should have apologised for that. I didn't... it wasn't quite the right thing to say.'

'No, it wasn't,' he agreed.

'Well, I'm sorry. OK?' Rebecca got out quickly.

'It was very,' he paused, 'ego-bruising.'

'Big ego, big bruise,' Rebecca murmured, her lashes fluttering upwards of their own accord, so that she met his dark blue gaze again.

'So it would seem.'

'I *have* apologised,' she reminded him breathily.

'And I would have said the pawing was pretty mutual, wouldn't you, Becca?'

The softly deep way he said her name sent shivers of sensual anticipation tingling along the length of her spine, and she swallowed convulsively, her mouth feeling suddenly dry and raw.

'I told you I was ... I was ...'

Byron raised that expressively mobile eyebrow in interested enquiry.

'I was tired. And vulnerable,' she finished hoarsely.

'Are you tired now?' His voice had dropped incredibly, incitingly lower.

'No.' The denial came out on an expelled breath.

'Then still vulnerable?'

Vulnerable? Good grief! If he only knew just how susceptible she was to his nearness. One touch and she was ready to meet him caress for caress, kiss for kiss, touch for ...

'Byron, please——' Her voice broke, a soft, choking sob.

'Please no or please yes?' His own voice sounded even, in control, but the pulse beating at one corner of his mouth betrayed him. For all his outward calm, Rebecca sensed that he was as aroused as she was.

His hand still gripping her wrist, he moved her arm behind her back, forcing her to turn slightly so that her breasts were against his hard body, her thighs meeting his. Her free hand went to his chest to try to put some space between them, but when her fingers encountered his firm flesh through the thin material of his shirt, felt the steadily accelerating beat of his heart, her body betrayed her, all restraint dissolving without even the merest attempt at resistance.

The amusement had faded from his eyes and had been replaced by that same raging fire she knew was reflected in her own eyes. One touch and she was aflame, flaring out of control. They stood poised like that, powerless to stop the rising passion that threatened to engulf them in a fiery burst.

So caught up in the intensity of the moment were they that when the back door opened and Jock stepped inside they drew apart in slow motion, like toys with run-down batteries. Jock stopped in surprise, his gaze going from one to the other before a broad smile lit his face.

'I sure hope I'm not interrupting anything. Should I go out and come in again?'

The sound of Jock's voice brought Rebecca back to earth with a jolt. She took another step away from Byron, her face burning with embarrassment.

'We were discussing my need, or lack of need, for a walking stick,' Byron remarked drily, and Jock laughed, slapping the younger man on the back.

'Is that what it was? Funny, didn't call it that in my day. Glad to see you two are getting along so well.' He turned back to Rebecca and she drew herself together with as much dignity as she could muster.

'If you'll both go through to the dining-room, I'll serve up the meal before it's burnt to a crisp,' she said sharply, and Jock chuckled as he followed Byron out of the kitchen.

'How does your parents' decision to remain in London pose a problem?' Rebecca asked Byron. She had scarcely tasted her meal, and now they were sitting over their coffee. Byron had just mentioned his mother's letter to Jock. 'I mean, if they're enjoying themselves——' She shrugged.

'My mother's worried having Kym under Laurel's feet for so long will be too much for my sister. Mum thinks a teenage boy, as well as three youngsters, Laurel's two and Tammy, is asking too much of Laurel's good nature. And I agree with Mum wholeheartedly. Laurel does need a break.' Byron sighed. 'So Mum has suggested that it would do Kym the world of good to come and stay here on the farm under my watchful eye for a couple of months.'

Rebecca nodded thoughtfully. 'Your mother may be right. Perhaps a change of scene, working on the farm, might give him a bit of breathing space.'

Byron looked sceptical.

'What will the young fellow think of coming to work on the farm?' asked Jock.

'According to Mum, Kym will think it's a great idea.' Byron pulled a face. 'Maybe he will agree to come over to Bay Ridge, but as to the working part of the arrangement—well, that remains to be seen.' Byron poured himself another cup of coffee. 'I've yet to see Kym lift a finger to get out of his own way.'

'I still think you're being too hard on him,' Rebecca told him. 'Seventeen's very young to be cast straight into university.'

'Hard or not,' Byron grimaced, 'it appears I'm going to be stuck with him. I would have insisted he come over here earlier, but Kym and I don't exactly hit it off.' He frowned reflectively. 'However, Laurel and Bill do need to have their house to themselves for a while, so Kym is going to have to make the best of Bay Ridge.'

'We can always use an extra hand,' Jock said as he climbed to his feet. 'I think I'll be off to bed. My old bones are tired tonight. Night, Becca. Thanks for dinner. See you, Will.'

When Jock left, Rebecca began to clear away their coffee-cups. She waited while Byron drained his.

'You know, it will make more work for you,' he remarked as he handed her the empty cup.

'Not that much, surely? I'll just add another potato to the pot,' she smiled quickly. Their isolation was setting her pulses racing again.

Byron followed her though into the kitchen and picked up the letter again, turning a couple of pages as she stacked the cups in the dishwasher.

'Mum said she was writing to Laurel as well, but I think I'll give her a ring. Laurel will probably try to insist Kym's no trouble because she's aware that relations between Kym and I are cool to say the least. Kym can come back with us when we fly over to collect Tammy.'

Rebecca turned to stare at him. 'We?' she queried.

'What? Oh, yes. You and I.' He was rereading part of his letter. 'Didn't I tell you?'

'No, you didn't.' Rebecca lifted her chin indignantly as he refolded the sheets and slipped them back into the envelope.

'I think it might be best if we pick up Tammy together. We'll stay the night with Laurel and Bill and come back on the ferry,' he informed her matter-of-factly. 'I promised Tammy a trip on the *Troubridge*, and I have a few special supplies and parts to see about, so I can have them shipped over at the same time.'

'But I can't just——' Rebecca stopped. 'I really can't see what difference it makes if I meet Tammy here or in Port Lincoln.'

'I discussed it with Laurel when I told her you'd be looking after Tammy. She agreed it would be better for Tammy to meet you in a familiar environment.' He was frowning a trifle distractedly. 'Apart from that, you can get to know Tammy while the three of us are together. When we get back to Bay Ridge I'll be out working all day, so I'll be leaving you on your own with Tammy. This way, she can get used to you while I'm around. I think it's the best idea, don't you?'

He did have a point, she realised. The little girl might feel more inclined to accept Rebecca if Byron was there to help them over the initial 'getting to know each other' period.

But for heaven's sake, she didn't want to fly to Port Lincoln with him, having him near her, meeting his sister and his young brother. It was all snowballing from a simple job of babysitting into...into...well, it was all getting far too complicated.

Byron Willoughby was too attractive, too potently magnetic, and she had a vertiginous feeling of being drawn into him, into a whirlpool of out-of-control emotions. She wasn't ready for them. Or Byron. And she hurriedly excused herself and escaped to her bedroom.

CHAPTER FIVE

THE aeroplane landed smoothly at Port Lincoln Airport, and Rebecca had to smother a sigh of relief. She'd never spent a longer few hours. In the confines of the small plane from Kangaroo Island to Adelaide Byron Willoughby was far too close to her, his body larger than life. Or so her fanciful imaginings told her. Even the more roomy Fokker Friendship on their flight down to Port Lincoln hadn't seemed to make it any easier to sit beside him.

And she still hadn't been able to shake the feeling of being induced into a situation she knew she should be avoiding at all cost. She felt somewhat akin to a fly being drawn into a spider's web, only it was no accidental snare. She knew what she was doing, where she was heading, and yet she continued to walk right on in. She seemed incapable of stopping herself.

Down on the tarmac Byron took her arm, guiding her across to the terminus. His hand on her elbow burned through the thickness of her red sweater and she shivered, pulling the loose black sleeveless jerkin which matched her slacks more tightly about her. The wind held a chill even in the bright sunshine, she told herself.

Inside the terminus, out of the stiff breeze, he excused himself to collect their luggage, and Rebecca ran her hand over her hair, hoping the wind hadn't left it too wild and woolly. Byron was back in no time, and set their cases down on the floor as he scanned the reception area for his sister. He glanced at his wristwatch.

'Just like Laurel to be late,' he remarked drily. 'I can't remember her ever arriving anywhere on time. She even kept poor Bill waiting at the altar for twenty minutes.'

Rebecca's gaze followed his, and her stomach churned nervously at the impending meeting with Byron's sister. What would she be like? She was a couple of years younger than Byron, he'd told her on the plane, and her husband, Bill, was a doctor, a GP.

'Ah!' Byron let out a satisfied ejaculation, and Rebecca saw a tall, dark-haired girl dashing towards them.

'Byron!' she cried delightedly as she threw her arms around him. He bore her salutations manfully, smiling indulgently down at her.

'I'm late again, aren't I?' she grinned ruefully. 'But Bill was called out just as we were leaving, and then the wretched car wouldn't start. Kym had to push it. I thought I'd never make it here.' She kissed Byron on the cheek and turned eagerly to Rebecca. 'And you have to be Rebecca. Hi! I'm Laurel Denning. Byron tells me you're going to look after Tammy for him.'

'Yes, for a while,' Rebecca began, and a faint, surprised shadow passed over the other girl's face. The striking features were very similar to her brother's, but in Laurel they were softer and undeniably feminine.

'Tammy's really looking forward to going home with you,' she told Rebecca. 'She misses Byron so much. It's great that he's found someone to look after her at last. Not that we don't love having her with us, but as far as Tammy's concerned there's no one like her father.'

Byron bent to pick up their cases. 'Let's get going,' he suggested, effectively ending the conversation. 'I suppose you've left the car in a no-parking zone as usual, Laurel?'

They climbed into Laurel's small white sedan, Byron slipping into the driver's seat without even consulting his sister, and Rebecca grimaced to herself. Typical. Overbearing male chauvinist.

'I usually let Byron drive,' said Laurel, as though she'd read Rebecca's mind, and as they pulled away from the airport she turned a little sideways in the front seat so that she could talk to Rebecca. 'I'm much more relaxed if Byron takes the wheel. Not that I'm a bad driver,' she laughed, 'it's just that having my brother as a passenger always seems to bring out the worst in me. I tend to crunch gears, inadvertently cut other drivers off, and generally make a thorough nuisance of myself. Much easier to let Byron command the ship.'

Byron pulled a face at her. 'You're just plain lazy and love being chauffeured.'

'Well, it does leave Rebecca and me free to talk.' She smiled at Rebecca with Byron's smile. 'I believe you were a secretary in Sydney before you returned to Kangaroo Island.'

Rebecca nodded. 'Yes. I started out in Adelaide working for Jameson's Electronics, and when they amalgamated and moved their head office to Sydney I went with them.'

'Sounds like a great job.'

'Yes, it was.' Rebecca told her. 'It was quite interesting. I was private secretary to one of the company's executives.' And would have been his mistress if Paul Drewett had had his way, she thought cynically to herself.

'What made you give it up?' Laurel was asking, and she must have seen some of Rebecca's soul-searching reflected in her eyes. 'If you don't mind my asking, that is. Tell me to mind my own business if you like.'

Rebecca laughed at Laurel's easy manner, but she wasn't able to prevent herself from glancing quickly at Byron. She'd revealed far too much to him the other night. 'I guess I'd just had enough of the hustle and bustle of city life,' she replied to his sister, wishing that had been the only reason for her return, but knowing

she had been running away from the relationship her
boss had wanted. 'So,' she shrugged, 'I came home to
the island.'

Her eyes returned to the back of Byron's head, to the
firm, tanned skin, the neatly trimmed dark hair that felt
soft to her fingers' touch. Home to Bay Ridge, which
wasn't her home any longer and never would be again.
Bay Ridge was Byron Willoughby's home now.

Rebecca was unaware that Laurel saw her eyes shift
to Byron, and she was equally oblivious of the speculative gleam in the other girl's eyes.

'Kangaroo Island's wonderfully rejuvenating, isn't it?'
Laurel commented conversationally. 'The pace of life is
so much more relaxed and unpressured. Our place is
usually such a mess of comings and goings, I sometimes
think I'll go mad. I find that at moments like that, once
a day at least, I think of Byron's farm as nothing short
of Utopia.'

'That's funny,' Byron put in wryly. 'I would have said
you brought your own mad pace with you when you
visited Bay Ridge.'

Laurel gave him a retaliatory jab in the ribs.

Byron was driving into the outskirts of the town now,
for the airport was some miles out of Port Lincoln, and
it wasn't long before they pulled into the driveway of a
strikingly modern brick home. The large front lawn was
beautifully kept, and a profusion of multicoloured
flowers grew in garden beds along the fences, paths and
on either side of the front entrance. Two large hanging
pots by the door overflowed masses of pink and mauve
petunias. Rebecca remarked on the flowers as she
climbed from the car.

'My one passion when I get a few spare moments,'
Laurel laughed. 'Come on in and meet the kids and Kym,
that's if the little angels haven't driven him crazy by now.
I left him in command, poor thing.' She shot a slightly
worried frown in Byron's direction.

Rebecca followed Laurel across the brick-paved entrance to the front door, leaving Byron to get their cases out of the boot. Inside was a small foyer, divided from the living-room on the left by a waist-high brick feature wall on which sat a tub of green fernery. The living-room itself was large and open with a high, timber-beamed cathedral ceiling and a centrally placed free-standing fireplace. Comfort went hand in hand with a pleasant décor of subdued tonings, and Rebecca thought she'd never seen a more restful room in her life, the sort of room one could settle peacefully into at the end of a trying day.

She said as much to Laurel, to the other girl's obvious pleasure.

'By the time I get to the living-room after my pandemonic days, I'm too exhausted to do more than fall asleep over my book,' she said. 'And talking about those sorts of days, I can't hear anything.' She frowned. 'I don't like it when they're quiet. What can they be up to?'

A stifled giggle came from the living-room, and Laurel strode around to lean over the back of one of the stuffed lounge chairs.

'Out of there, Jamie,' she said firmly, and dexterously hauled a dark-haired four-year-old into the open.

'Oh, Mummy,' he protested indignantly. 'Now Uncle Kym will find me and then I'll be up.'

At that moment Byron walked through the door behind Rebecca and set their cases down on the tiled floor. The little boy squirmed out of his mother's hold and raced across the floor.

'Uncle Byron!' he yelled loudly, laughing delightedly as Byron swung him up in the air and then deposited him back on the floor again.

Jamie's yell brought the carpet-muffled thumping of running feet as two little girls raced through from the back of the house. 'Uncle Byron!' 'Daddy!' they cried in unison.

Rebecca's eyebrows rose as Byron seemed to be swamped by children. The two little girls were of an age, both dark-haired, although one had short, loose curls and the other straight hair caught in pigtails tied with red ribbons.

Laurel stepped forward and spoke above the babble of little voices.

'Jamie, Peta. Go find Uncle Kym and tell him we're home,' she said, and the little boy and the little girl with pigtails turned and disappeared along the hallway.

The little girl with the dark brown curls clung to Byron's arm as she turned to smile shyly at Rebecca. Rebecca searched for a resemblance to her father, but could find none in the piquant little face, apart from large dark blue eyes. Yes, perhaps the eyes were Byron's.

'Rebecca, this is Tammy,' Byron said evenly. 'Tammy, meet Rebecca.'

'Hello, Tammy.' With Byron and Laurel looking on, Rebecca felt just as shy as the little girl appeared to be.

'Hello, Rebecca,' Tammy said softly.

'Rebecca's going to be staying with us at Bay Ridge,' Byron told her, and Tammy nodded.

'I know. Aunt Laurel told me Rebecca was going to look after me and take me to school.'

Rebecca smiled, wanting to say something reassuring to the child but unable to think of a thing. Having no dealings with children, she felt at a loss. She'd known it would be like this.

'Will you make my breakfast, too, like Aunt Laurel does?' Tammy asked, her blue eyes on Rebecca's face.

'Yes, I will. You'll have to tell me all about the things you like to eat,' she said lamely.

'I don't like sausages,' Tammy informed her solemnly.

'We found him! We found him!' Peta and Jamie came running back down the hallway, followed more slowly by Kym Willoughby.

At seventeen, he showed signs of being every bit as attractive as his brother, although he was somewhat shorter and slimmer than Byron. Kym had the same dark hair, which he wore a little longer than Rebecca would have thought was in vogue these days with his contemporaries, but he was dressed in the inevitable jeans and T-shirt. At the moment his mouth turned down sulkily and he slouched, his hands shoved in his pockets.

'Kym, come and meet Rebecca,' Laurel said, her tone carrying a mild rebuke that didn't seem to go down too well with the young man, if Kym's expression was anything to go by.

'Hello.' Rebecca smiled at him. She felt some sympathy for him, for she saw her brother Rudy in the young boy's silent dissension. Rudy had often looked just like that after a session with Jock.

'Hi!' Kym replied, his eyes sliding from Rebecca to his brother and back again. 'Hi, big brother.' Kym's tone bordered on the deprecatory, and Rebecca sensed the tension in the man beside her. 'Long time no see.'

'Hello, Kym,' Byron replied evenly. 'Good to see you.'

'I'll bet.' Kym smiled crookedly, but Byron refused to be drawn.

'Which rooms are we in, Laurel?' He turned to his sister. 'I'll take these cases upstairs.'

'You'll have to share the end room with Kym, and I've put Rebecca in the green room.'

'Fine.' Byron started up the stairs to the right.

Kym's eyes momentarily followed his brother and then returned to Rebecca to sweep her in a totally different, almost insolent manner. To her annoyance Rebecca felt hot colour flood her face, and she had an irrational urge to slap Byron's young brother.

'I'll pop into the kitchen and make us a cup of coffee.' Laurel smiled easily. 'Tammy, why don't you take Rebecca through to the dining-room? Uncle Kym, Peta and Jamie can help me in the kitchen.' She shepherded the two children before her and took her brother's arm as she passed him, not giving him the option of debating her suggestion.

Tammy smiled at Rebecca and took her hand. 'Come this way, Rebecca,' she said with shy importance.

Rebecca allowed herself to be guided through the arched doorway under the stairs that led into the dining-room. It was also luxuriously furnished, but still remained a practical family room.

'Would you like to sit here?' Tammy asked formally, and pulled out a chair for Rebecca.

'Thank you.' She sat down. 'How about sitting beside me so we can talk?'

Tammy nodded and slid on to the chair Rebecca indicated.

'What a nice room,' Rebecca said, just a little discomposed by the child's grave regard.

'Yes. It's Aunt Laurel's favourite room,' she said. 'This is a very nice house——' she paused and looked levelly at Rebecca '—but I really like being at the farm with Daddy.'

'Then you must be looking forward to going home.'

'Oh, yes, I am.' She rested her chin on her hand. 'Will you truly be taking me to school?' she asked Rebecca seriously, and Rebecca nodded.

'Yes. Your father would like you to attend the school on the island. What do you think about that?'

Tammy gave it a moment's thought. 'I like school here, but I want to go to the one on the island because then I can be with Daddy all the time.' Her blue eyes fixed on Rebecca. 'Will you play with me sometimes and help me with my reading? I'm not very good at reading,' she confided.

'If you'd like me to.'

'Will you cook breakfast for Daddy, too?'

Rebecca nodded.

'And dinner?'

'Yes.' Rebecca laughed. 'I'll be cooking for everybody.'

'And do the washing like Aunt Laurel?'

'I guess so.'

'And will you read me stories sometimes?'

'Yes.'

'At bedtime?'

'Yes.'

'You mean you'll be living right in our house with Daddy and me, and not just come each day like Mary did?' Tammy's little face lit up, and her beaming smile showed the gap of a lost front tooth.

'Yes, I'll be living in the house,' she told the little girl.

'Oh.' Tammy gave a happy sigh. 'Are you going to be my new Mummy, then? Really Mummys and Daddys live in the same house, don't they?'

Rebecca was completely taken aback by the child's question and, looking at the glowing smile on the pretty little face, she knew an absurd urge to say, yes, that she wanted nothing more than to mother this child, to care for her. And her father.

But she hadn't answered the little girl's question, and she had to somehow make it clear to the child that she'd made a mistake. How should she handle it?

She heard a movement behind her and turned to see Byron filling the doorway. How long had he been there? Had he heard his daughter? Her eyes met his, searched for his reaction, but he was regarding her through half-closed lids, his expression shuttered. Rebecca felt a soft colour flood her cheeks as he strode forward and sat down at the end of the table facing his daughter.

'I guess Aunt Laurel has explained that Rebecca will be staying at Bay Ridge to look after us?' he asked softly, and Tammy nodded. 'You know I have to be out working on the farm each day, so Rebecca is going to be there to be company for you.'

'And she's going to live with us,' Tammy told him firmly.

'She'll be staying in our house, yes,' Byron agreed.

'Is she going to be my new mother?' the little girl persisted, much to Rebecca's mortification. 'You know I'd like that, Daddy. Remember, I told you?'

'Yes, I remember, sweetie,' Byron answered her matter-of-factly. 'But for Rebecca to be your mother she'd have to marry me.'

'Like Aunt Laurel and Uncle Bill?' Tammy put in.

'Mmm. And people get married because they love each other very much.'

'And do you love Rebecca very much?' Tammy asked, her blue eyes going hopefully from Rebecca back to her father.

'Rebecca and I haven't known each other very long, so Rebecca will just be our babysitter, like Mary was, except Rebecca will be there all the time,' he explained.

'Oh.' Tammy sighed loudly, her eyes resting sadly on Rebecca. She turned back to Byron. 'I like Rebecca.'

'That's great.' Byron smiled. 'You can get to be good friends.'

Tammy pursed her lips, looking as though she was about to pursue the subject, but the door from the kitchen swung open and Laurel escorted her two children into the room, keeping a wary eye on the plate of scones in one small hand and the sugar bowl in another.

'Put them carefully on the table,' she directed as she set down her tray of pottery coffee mugs and a matching coffee-pot.

Kym followed her with a tray of drinks for the children. Laurel's glance smilingly encompassed them all before she began to pour the coffee.

After a light lunch, Laurel suggested they have a swim in the pool in the back yard of the house, and when Rebecca shivered visibly at the thought, Laurel told her the pool was heated and that it was fenced against the wind. Brushing aside Rebecca's protest that she hadn't brought a swimsuit with her, Byron's sister found her a bikini and sent them all to their rooms to change.

The bikini wasn't exactly a perfect fit, Rebecca grimaced as she stood in front of the full-length white-edged mirror fixed on the wall in her room, and told herself she couldn't possibly wear the skimpy outfit in public.

The bikini briefs fitted quite well, displayed her long, nicely shaped legs to perfection, but the top was a size too small. At least, that was what it looked like to Rebecca. The bra top was cut low over her full breasts, and showed a faint line between the white and tanned skin left by her own more modest bikini. This one was far too revealing.

A tap sounded on the door and Rebecca drew a sharp breath.

'Rebecca? It's Laurel. How does the bikini fit?'

Rebecca let out the breath she held and crossed to the door.

'I think it's a bit too, well——' she began as Laurel stepped inside.

'Rubbish!' exclaimed Laurel before Rebecca could finish. 'It looks great.' She glanced down regretfully at herself. 'You're just the right height. Look at me, all legs and practically no shape at all.'

Rebecca thought Laurel was being a little hard on herself. She had a neat, trim figure and she told Laurel so. But Laurel brushed that aside.

'I'd give anything for a few more curves like you,' she added.

Rebecca ran her hand over the bikini top, wishing she wasn't quite so well endowed. 'I don't know, Laurel,' she frowned.

'Come on, the bikini's fine,' Laurel assured her. 'But I feel I should warn you, if my Bill comes home, expect to be ogled. Bill's definitely a boob man. Heaven knows why he married me,' she added ruefully.

Rebecca laughed and turned back to pick up her towel.

'Ah, Byron, you're ready,' she heard Laurel say, and Rebecca's body stiffened instinctively. 'So are we.'

'I'd like a word with Rebecca before we go down, if you don't mind, Laurel.' Byron said to his sister, and to Rebecca's embarrassment Laurel gave a softly teasing laugh.

'Of course not. Seeing Rebecca in that bikini, I can understand why you want her to yourself for a while. See you both down at the pool whenever.'

Rebecca stood stiffly inside the room, her towel clutched in her nerveless fingers, as Byron stepped inside. His eyes engulfed her in one swift, all-encompassing glance, and she knew those sharp eyes had not missed a fraction of her.

'I'd like to talk to you. Just for a moment,' he said, and his deeply low voice teased her unmercifully.

Of their own accord, her wide eyes slid down the long, all but naked length of him, down from his broad shoulders to the lightly curling mat of dark hair on his chest that arrowed downwards over his flat stomach to the brief, dark blue swimming trunks he wore.

Rebecca's mouth went dry and her heartbeats began the now familiar erratic tattoo. He was almost too attractive to be believed, she thought hysterically, and then had to pull herself forcefully together, for Byron was speaking.

'I'd like to apologise for Tammy,' he said unsmilingly. 'For embarrassing you this morning.'

'Oh, no. That's all right. Really,' Rebecca hastened to convince him, and she gave an attempt at a laugh to lighten the undertow of gathering tension that was flowing between them, drawing them both out of their depth. 'I understand how she came to get the wrong idea.'

His eyelashes fell to shield the brooding look he was giving her, and she sensed but didn't comprehend his sudden displeasure. She shifted nervously, her body growing hot under his regard.

Byron frowned and turned slightly away from her, his hands resting on his hips, and, mesmerised, Rebecca watched the play of his muscles as he moved.

'I've tried to do the best for Tammy. When we were together in Melbourne I was very careful, even circumspect,' he grimaced, 'when it came to my women friends. But I guess Tammy feels insecure as things stand, maybe a little more insecure than I'd realised.' He frowned reflectively. 'I thought being here in the family situation with Laurel and Bill would have been enough to overcome that, but perhaps it hasn't. Obviously it hasn't.'

Rebecca moved closer to him, understanding his concern and admiring him for being aware of the problems involved in raising his daughter single-handedly.

'It's only natural for a child to compare her situation with those of the other children she mixes with,' she told him compassionately.

'I suppose so.' He ran a hand through his hair. 'But somehow I still feel a certain sense of failure.'

'I can understand that,' she said huskily, 'but you shouldn't. You can't change what's happened in the past, no matter how much you may want to alter it.'

Rebecca's hand went out spontaneously to touch his arm in a purely sympathetic gesture, and he turned his head slowly to look down at her through lash-shielded eyes. She felt his body grow still, and her fingers trembled slightly against his smooth skin.

Realising what she was doing, she drew her hand away as though she'd been stung. Touching him had been a mistake. It only intensified the current of awareness that skittered between them, surging so very close to the surface.

'Becca.' Her name seemed to be drawn painfully from him and he caught her hand in one of his, carrying it back to the warm, bare skin of his chest, holding her fingers against him.

Her eyes went to where his strong, tanned hand covered hers, then rose to meet his eyes, and she felt her knees turn to water. If she moved, she knew her legs would give way beneath her.

The silent, burning message in the blue depths of Byron's gaze, in the sensual curve of his mouth, filled her with an escalating yearning that swept over her, threatening to thrust aside her self-control. She actually felt herself leaning, compelled, towards him, wanting desperately to feel his naked flesh against hers, knowing he wanted just that, wanted it as much as she did, when the sound of a door closing cut the air with a brutal suddenness.

CHAPTER SIX

FOOTSTEPS approached, faltered, moved again. Kym's 'Excuse me', delivered in an exaggerated tone, said that he had seen them standing close together, Byron's hand clasping Rebecca's against his chest, that he had assessed the situation and read it correctly, and had found it quite amusing. Rebecca stepped quickly, guiltily, backwards, pulling her hand from beneath Byron's. Kym's footsteps continued down the hall, and he was whistling tunelessly as he started down the stairs.

Byron's face glowered after his young brother, and then he turned back to Rebecca. 'Becca——' he began throatily.

Drawing a deep, steadying breath, she put more space between them. 'You go on down. I won't be a minute.'

For long, nerve-stretching moments he stood watching her with that same shrouded intensity before he turned away and strode down the hallway in Kym's wake.

Rebecca sank down on the bed and covered her face with her hands. The whole scene couldn't have taken more than minutes, but she felt washed out, as though she'd stumbled out of a long, fatiguing ordeal.

And she had to put a stop to it. This emotion-charged situation with Byron was bad enough as it was, actually existing between them, but when other people began to get involved it became intolerable to Rebecca. It had started on the island with Jock and his knowing smiles, and now Laurel and Kym were becoming part of it.

To make matters worse, they all had the wrong end of the stick. Clearly they were under the misapprehension that there was some sort of relationship between herself and Byron. But they were mistaken. They were, she impressed on herself.

Anything that had happened between herself and Byron Willoughby was purely physical, she told herself, just the result of certain coinciding circumstances. Her emotions were topsy-turvy at present because she'd left the security of her job, come home to her grandfather, the returning prodigal, only to find her home had been sold. She was bound to be in a susceptible state.

While Byron—well, it was blatantly obvious that he was a very virile man. She grimaced at her expression. Hadn't he admitted himself when he was discussing Tammy that he'd kept his romances away from the child's impressionable eyes? A sensation very much like painful jealousy gripped her, and she bit off a self-derisive imprecation.

So he had had relationships. Hundreds, for all Rebecca knew. It was none of her business if he kept a harem, she told herself. The trouble was that Byron and herself had been thrown together, and living on Bay Ridge wouldn't have given him much opportunity for indulging in the usual diversions with the opposite sex. The whole thing was a simple study in proximity.

Had she met Byron in another place, at another time, it would never have happened. They most probably wouldn't have noticed each other. He might have caught her eye, being so tall and good-looking, but as for being attracted to him, it was laughable.

You're kidding yourself, an inner voice jeered. You don't even begin to believe that. You would have felt this attraction to him no matter where or when your lives crossed.

Rebecca stood up angrily, annoyed with herself. Thinking this way, dwelling on it, was childish. She was an adult, not a lovesick teenager.

Love. Her thoughts shied away from the word like a startled colt. It wasn't love. No way! Love was a more subdued, gentler emotion. Love wasn't this heated, burning attraction, this almost overwhelming need to reach out and touch, this growing fever of desire to...

Rebecca ran her hand distractedly through her hair. Never love. It was pure, unadulteratedly sexual, physical attraction. But never love. Love had nothing to do with it.

Had she been a different type of person, had she been used to having casual affairs, she could have done just that: had an affair with him, got him out of her system, and then put it all behind her. Forgotten him.

Her body trembled at the mere thought of making love with Byron Willoughby, of his hands touching her body caressingly, of his lips moving over her mouth, her throat... and of her ultimate surrender.

My God! She shook her head. What was wrong with her? She seemed to have a one-track mind, and it all led back to Byron Willoughby.

Slowly, almost dazedly, she walked out of the room and down the hallway. She wasn't going to allow herself to indulge in a sordid affair, she told herself firmly. If she'd wanted that, her ex-boss would have been more than happy to oblige. She supposed she was out-of-date, but she didn't believe in sex for sex's sake, and she wasn't going to start changing her whole outlook now. No matter how potently attractive Byron was.

She was just going to have to cope with it as best she could, and the first thing she'd have to do was ensure that Byron and she spent as little time as possible alone together. That should be easier now that Tammy and Kym were coming back to the farm with them.

Yes, if she nipped this attraction in the bud, life would settle down and she could do a conscientious job of caring for Tammy until Byron found a permanent baby-sitter. And then she'd move on. She totally suppressed the probing sliver of doubt that tried to tell her she'd already left leaving too late, that Byron Willoughby was by now a part of her, as necessary to her as food and drink.

At least her soul-searching thoughts took her mind off her reticence about joining the family in the pool, and she was in the water, taking part in a strenuous Rafferty's Rules game of water polo, before she knew it. Byron was in the pool, too, her body was very aware of that, but he was keeping his distance.

Only once did he come close, reaching over her head from behind to catch the ball, ducking her. Rebecca came to the surface, spluttering, and his strong arms held her, his skin searing her smooth, wet flesh until she'd recovered her breath, and then he moved to the other end of the pool, a gaping chasm away from her.

The afternoon flew by, and somewhat to her surprise Rebecca enjoyed herself. Later on Laurel's husband, Bill, arrived home. He was of medium height with slightly thinning dark hair, and Rebecca put his age in the early forties. He looked a little tired, but smiled happily at his wife.

'A perfect set of twins,' he told Laurel after the introductions to Rebecca had been made.

Laurel and Bill were smiling, momentarily lost in each other, and Rebecca found herself sighing softly. The couple obviously had a good marriage. There were no undercurrents, and Laurel evidently understood the demands of Bill's work. Love showed in their eyes as they exchanged glances. That was what love was all about.

And Rebecca was still thinking about Laurel and Bill as she dressed for the barbecue Laurel had decided they'd have. It must be wonderful to feel secure in the knowledge that you loved and were loved. Perhaps her own parents had looked at each other that way.

Her thoughts then slid immediately to Byron, and she paused in the act of pulling her dress over her head. She stood immobile for tense moments before she slowly lowered her dress, zipped it up and smoothed the skirt over her hips. Her reflection shimmered back at her from the mirror, her eyes bright and dark and totally alive. Only one person was responsible for their burning glow.

Rebecca turned quickly away from the mirror, chiding herself irritably for being fanciful again. At the first opportunity she must speak to Byron about getting another babysitter for Tammy. With each hour that passed she felt she was being drawn more tightly, deeper into the web, and she could only foresee more pain for herself. Self-inflicted pain, at that.

It was obvious Byron was attracted to her, but a brief sexual interlude would be abandoned when the first fiery glow died down. She wanted far more than that. She wanted the shared smile, the touch of an affectionate hand. And she wanted forever. Understanding the way Byron still felt about his late wife, she knew she was crying for the moon.

Resolutely she pushed a rush of despression to the back of her mind and left her room. As she walked downstairs she adjusted the elasticised cuffs of her dress, knowing the soft apple-green colour complemented her dark colouring. The long, slightly full sleeves and high, loosely rolled neckline should keep her warm in the chill of the evening breeze off the bay. She glanced downwards. The bodice fitted over her breasts and the skirt fell from gathers at the waist beneath a narrow belt.

With the dress she wore white strapless high-heeled shoes, and she'd taken especial care over her make-up. Her dark hair, newly washed after the afternoon in the pool, shone glossily, and its loose, natural curls cascaded to her shoulders.

She found her way to the kitchen, where Laurel was tossing a fresh salad in a huge bowl.

'Hello. Anything I can do to help?' Rebecca asked a little shyly.

'Welcome.' Laurel laughed. 'When it comes to cooking, I need all the help I can get. But at least I can't burn a salad, and as Bill's going to be cooking out at the barbecue——' She shrugged expressively. 'There!' She set the bowl aside. 'Now all we have to do is take everything outside. You can give me a hand to do that if you like.'

'Right.' Rebecca picked up a dish of sweetcorn and one of diced tomato, onion and celery. 'Just lead the way.'

'We'll put everything on this table,' Laurel said as they stepped out on to the patio, 'and then everyone can help themselves.'

They soon had the smorgasbord ready, and Laurel went inside to fetch a tray of glasses.

The patio was covered by almost transparent corrugated roofing sheets, and the lighting was well placed and unobtrusive. Bill was already at the barbecue, and the three children sat on tall stools off to the side, talking to him. Rebecca joined them.

Bill turned and smiled at her, his cheeks slightly pink from bending over the heated plate, and he wore a huge chef's apron with cartoon-like characters adorning it, proclaiming him to be the world's greatest cook.

'Just about ready to start cooking,' he said, waving his long barbecue fork around. 'How does madam like her steak?'

'Well done, please,' Rebecca said quickly.

'Well done I can handle,' Bill grinned and his gaze went past Rebecca. 'That's about all I can manage on this barbecue, isn't it, Byron?'

Rebecca turned slowly to the side as Byron joined them, and she was unable to prevent her eyes from rising to meet his. Her entire nervous system tingled in unison with her heartbeats, and she tore her gaze from his in case he read her feelings in her eyes.

'You do a great job, Bill, and you know it, so no false modesty.' Byron laughed, and Rebecca let her eyes slide surreptitiously over his neat, dark blue trousers and his cream, shoulder-hugging, short-sleeved towelling shirt.

His hand came out to rest lightly, oh, so casually, on Rebecca's shoulder, and her breath caught painfully in her chest.

'Don't let him fool you, Becca.' His voice was filled with amusement. 'If Bill hadn't been a doctor, he could quite easily have ended up a chef.'

'Luckily for me,' put in Laurel as she joined them, and Rebecca knew she hadn't missed noticing Byron's proprietorial hand on her shoulder. 'Can I drag you away to open the wine, brother dear?' she asked teasingly.

'If you insist.' Byron's gaze lingered on Rebecca for what seemed like interminable, tension-filled seconds before the corners of his mouth lifted ruefully and he moved away. Rebecca felt suddenly, inexplicably cold.

The meal was delicious, and they laughed and talked as they sat in the fresh night air. Kym switched on the stereo and Bill danced enthusiastically with the laughing children. Rebecca sat smilingly watching them until Kym grabbed her hand and pulled her to her feet. She tried to protest but he wasn't prepared to let her go, so she gave in and danced with him. He threw himself into it with much zest, and while privately Rebecca thought he was something of an exhibitionist, she had to admit he was a very good modern dancer.

Soon her leg muscles began to ache, and she protested to Kym and sat down to catch her breath, grimacing at him when he commented on 'old people being past it'.

Laurel's eyebrows rose. 'I don't know how our parents have managed to raise that boy, do you, Byron? It's a wonder someone hasn't done him in by now.'

Kym laughed and pulled Laurel to her feet to take Rebecca's place. When he forgot to be sulky, Rebecca reflected, Kym could be very likeable.

Only Laurel's empty chair separated Rebecca from Byron, but he might as well have been sitting close beside her, for her body clamoured at his nearness. She watched him out of the corner of her eye as he sat casually in his seat, long, muscular legs stretched out in front of him. Then he moved to take Laurel's place beside her and her body tensed. For a moment she thought her heart had ceased beating.

'I've booked us on tomorrow evening's ferry home,' he was saying. 'I'll be borrowing Laurel's car in the morning to check on my cargo. Is there anything you'd like to pick up while we're in Lincoln? Any shopping to do?'

'No, I don't think so. But,' Rebecca paused, 'it's about Rudy.'

'Your brother?'

Rebecca nodded. 'Jock said he was working on one of the tuna boats. I'd like to see him while I'm here, so perhaps you might drop me down at the jetty and I could ask around for him. Someone may have heard of him.'

'He was working on the *Almonta* when I met him here, but that was nearly a year ago. He may have moved on.'

'I know. But I'd like to try to find him.'

Byron regarded her for a moment and then nodded. 'I'll make some enquiries for you tomorrow.'

'There's no need to go to that trouble,' Rebecca hurriedly assured him. 'I can easily do it myself.'

'It's no trouble, Becca. I'll be going down there anyway. I'll take you.' He turned away from her as Bill sank wearily down beside them.

'I'm not as young as I used to be.' Bill dabbed at his damp brow with his handkerchief. 'Whatever became of the good old smoochy music?'

Eventually Laurel decided it was time for the children to go to bed, and they traipsed after her, making half-hearted and vain pleas to be allowed to stay up longer. Rebecca went with them and helped Tammy into her pyjamas. She watched her snuggle down into the bed. The little girl sighed sleepily, and as Rebecca bent to tuck in the covers her arms went around Rebecca's neck in a hug that almost overbalanced her.

'I like you already, Becca,' she said softly, automatically picking up the name she'd heard her father call Rebecca. 'I'm glad you'll be looking after Daddy and me.'

Rebecca smiled, her heart going out to the child, and she returned the cuddle, kissing Tammy on the forehead. 'I'm glad I will be, too,' she said softly, and meant it.

'All tucked up?' Laurel asked as Rebecca gently closed the bedroom door behind her, and Rebecca nodded.

'Aren't they adorable when they're asleep?' Laurel laughed. 'I so look forward to bedtime some days,' she added expressively. 'How about some coffee?'

They were in the kitchen now, and Rebecca set out the cups while Laurel brewed the coffee.

'Byron tells me you're going home on the *Troubridge* tomorrow,' Laurel remarked. 'I wish you could stay longer.'

'Yes, it would be nice, but Byron wants to get back to the farm. They're clearing the west paddock.' Rebecca set spoons on each saucer.

'He works himself too hard, but then again, he always has.' Laurel sighed. 'When he played football he threw himself into it to the exclusion of all else. It's no wonder he was such a good player, he was so dedicated.' She frowned. 'I did hope once he bought the farm he'd take some time to relax and enjoy life, but from what I can tell it's all work, work, work.'

'I'm afraid my grandfather let the farm get a bit run down because he couldn't manage it on his own, so I suppose Byron wants to get it into shape,' Rebecca suggested

'Mmm. I wish he would take it easier, though. I worry about him.' She smiled ruefully. 'Not that he'd thank me for interfering, but I'd appreciate it if you could talk him into going on a holiday or something like that.'

Rebecca glanced up in surprise. 'Oh, I don't think he'd be inclined to listen to me,' she told the other girl.

Laurel's eyes met Rebecca's speculatively and Rebecca felt herself flush. 'Honestly, Laurel, Byron and I scarcely know each other. I've only been back on the island a fortnight.'

A fortnight. Rebecca shocked herself. She'd only met Byron Willoughby two short weeks ago. And yet it seemed as though she'd known him all her life.

'Oh. How strange. I thought somehow you'd known each other for longer than that.' Laurel was looking at her piercingly. 'Byron knew your brother, didn't he? And I seem to remember he visited Kangaroo Island years ago, and couldn't stop talking about it.'

'Yes, I think he did. But he only met Rudy, my brother, here in Port Lincoln by chance, and Rudy mentioned then that Bay Ridge might have been up for sale.'

'Oh. And you never met Byron in Sydney?'

Rebecca's eyes flew wide in surprise. 'In Sydney? No, I didn't. What... what made you think that?'

Laurel shrugged. 'Byron made quite a few trips to Sydney on business. I just put two and two together and came up with a four that was way off beam. I had it wrong, didn't I?' Laurel seemed to pause momentarily before continuing, 'Then you didn't know Nikki, either?'

'Nikki?' Rebecca frowned.

'Byron's wife,' Laurel explained.

'No. No, I didn't.' A hundred questions flew into Rebecca's mind, but she stopped herself voicing any of them. She wanted to ask Laurel so many things, while part of her dreaded knowing any more about the woman Byron had loved and married. 'Tammy must miss her,' she added quickly, in case Laurel should recognise her curiosity.

'Oh, I don't think Tammy saw very much of her mother,' Laurel remarked drily. 'Nikki wasn't exactly the maternal type. You could have knocked me down with a feather when Byron told us Nikki was pregnant. She was Nikki Parsons before she married Byron. She got a lot of publicity when she was the Victorian representative in the Miss Australia Quest. Perhaps you've heard of her?'

Rebecca shook her head. 'No, I don't think I have.'

'She was a model, gorgeous-looking, tall and willowy with long, fair hair, and after the quest she went into TV hostessing.' Laurel shook her head. 'Very photogenic, and you'd have thought butter wouldn't melt in her mouth.'

Rebecca's eyebrows rose at the bitter tone in Laurel's voice.

'Oh, there was never any love lost between Nikki and me,' Laurel said emphatically. 'When she met Byron it was his third year with Carlton and he was their star player. Nikki got her hooks into him and she didn't let go. Their wedding even had TV coverage.'

'I suppose with Byron being such a good player his wedding was newsworthy,' Rebecca remarked, more for something to say. She could imagine the setting: flowers, confetti, a beautiful bride. And the groom.

'Oh, Nikki had her share of fans. She got loads of publicity in the beauty quest.' Laurel pulled a face. 'Even I have to admit she was pretty gorgeous-looking. But that didn't make her the best wife and mother. Nikki just wasn't cut out for domesticity. Byron should have known that.' Laurel shook her head ruefully. 'I guess I shouldn't be gossiping about it, should I?' She glanced thoughtfully at Rebecca. 'But as I see it, you'll be looking after Tammy so you should know something of her background. Tammy's a great kid, but she's dreadfully insecure. Nikki was never there for her, so from the time she was born Byron's been the only parent she's known. She needs to be with him again. She misses him so much, she has nightmares about it. Being back with her father should stop that.'

'Does she have the nightmares often?' Rebecca asked concernedly, pushing questioning thoughts about Byron's wife out of her mind.

'Not so often lately,' Laurel patted her arm. 'Don't go worrying about it. She'll be fine now, you'll see. Being with her father will make all the difference to Tammy.'

'I hope so. I've never really had much experience with children,' Rebecca told her.

'Nothing to it.' Laurel laughed at Rebecca's sceptical expression. 'You know, Rebecca, I think you're just what Byron needs. And Tammy, too,' she added quickly.

'Laurel, I——'

'OK. Enough said.' Laurel held up her hand. 'But you will try to get Byron to slow down, won't you? Maybe having Tammy with him will do the trick.' She turned to pick up the tray of steaming mugs. 'I just want to see my brother happy. He deserves it.'

Rebecca made no comment and they rejoined the men, Laurel passing around the coffee.

'I was about to come and rescue you both,' Byron remarked, his glance going from his sister to Rebecca. 'What took you so long?'

'We were talking about you, actually,' Laurel told him as Rebecca sat down next to Kym, apart from Byron. 'I was telling Rebecca you work too hard and that you should be thinking about taking a holiday. You haven't had one in years.'

'Now don't go clucking over me, Laurel,' Byron said good-naturedly. 'Strange as it may seem, I can look after myself.'

'We all need a break occasionally,' Laurel persevered.

'I know. And I intend to take it easy while Tammy gets used to being at Bay Ridge. I want to get her settled before she has to start at her new school.' Byron sipped his coffee.

'You do? That's great.' Laurel beamed. 'And it's not before time.'

'It's been a case of work to be done on Bay Ridge, and sitting around looking at it doesn't accomplish much,' he remarked drily. 'But now Kym's coming over that will be an extra pair of hands——'

'Oh, don't mind me,' Kym interrupted sarcastically. 'Just call me the slave labour.'

'Kym!' Laurel frowned at her younger brother.

'And will be a great help,' Byron finished, fixing Kym with a straight look, and Kym's gaze was the first to fall.

'Will you be taking those tractor parts back with you?' Bill asked, diplomatically changing the subject, and Byron nodded.

'I'll borrow Laurel's car in the morning, if I may, and check the order out. Tammy can come along, and Rebecca and I want to make some enquiries down at the jetty, about her brother. They haven't heard from him for some time.'

Rebecca's lips compressed. So he'd decided he was going to handle it all. It seemed he thought he could make a decision and everyone else was expected to fall into line with it. Her eyes warred with Byron's. Now it seemed she would be spending the morning with him as well. Why could he possibly want her along? To look after his daughter, an inner voice answered her. Why else? Why should she bring it down to the personal? This was simply a matter of employment.

'Your brother works on the tuna boats, doesn't he?' Bill had turned to Rebecca. 'No doubt someone will have word of him. You shouldn't have much trouble contacting him, unless he's at sea.'

'I don't think they've been out for a couple of days because of the weather,' Laurel put in. 'I hope you don't strike a bad trip on the ferry. Although it's not as windy today as it has been. How do you think it will be, Bill?' Laurel turned to her husband and he smiled at Byron.

'What can I say?' he appealed.

'Not much once Laurel starts,' Byron laughed.

Laurel gave him a quelling look and turned to Rebecca. 'Do you know Port Lincoln at all?' she asked, ignoring the two men.

'Not well, no. I have been here before, but that was years ago,' Rebecca answered.

'You'll notice the difference in it, then,' Laurel told her. 'You can't really see much in a day, but Byron can drive you around the town, give you a bit of a Cook's tour, if you like.'

'I hear there's talk of expanding the silos,' Byron remarked as Bill lit up his pipe, and the two men went on to discuss the situation.

Some time later Bill went inside to answer the telephone and Laurel began to gather up the cups to brew some more coffee. Byron waved Rebecca back into her seat when she went to follow Laurel into the kitchen, saying he would give Laurel a hand himself. That left Rebecca alone with Kym.

'Are you looking forward to coming over to stay on the farm?' she asked him.

Kym gave her what passed for a meaningful look and shrugged. 'It will be a change of a boring old scene.'

'Byron will be glad of the help, especially as he's clearing the west paddock.'

'I guess. But farming's not exactly my thing.'

'What is?'

He looked at her enquiringly.

'What is your thing?' Rebecca elaborated.

Kym shrugged. 'Who knows? Maybe nothing. I'd really like to get in some fishing, though. I hear it's great over on the island.' He gave her a crooked, cynical smile. 'But don't worry, Rebecca, I'll be helping Big Brother out. I mean, it's the least I can do for my bed and board. As long as I'm allotted my day of rest like the other peasants.'

If Kym was trying to be rude he was succeeding, and she forced down a wave of irritation because she sensed

he received some enjoyment out of knowing he was pro-
voking antipathy. Rebecca refused to rise to his bait.

'I'm sure Byron can use your assistance,' she said
blandly, and knew he was looking at her sharply, sus-
pecting from her tone that she was mocking him. 'Have
you ever worked on a farm before?'

'No.' Kym slouched back in his chair.

'What have you been doing since you left school?'

'Doing?' Kym queried in a slightly bored tone.

'You know, how do you spend your time?' Rebecca
felt like snapping at him. She was only trying to make
conversation with him for the sake of good manners,
and she was beginning to wonder why she was bothering.
'Did you play football, too?'

She didn't need to see the shuttered, sulky look on
Kym's face to know she'd said the wrong thing. It seemed
she'd inadvertently touched a raw nerve.

'Not me,' he replied shortly. 'One footballer in the
family's enough, don't you think? Besides, after Big
Brother's success, well, who could top that?' He chewed
on his bottom lip. 'Have you seen Byron play?'

'No.' Rebecca frowned. 'I was never a fan of the game
like my brother was.'

'Oh.' Kym was directing that same speculative look
at her. 'Didn't you know Byron when he played
football?'

'No.'

'Oh. I thought——' He paused and then shrugged,
and they were silent for a moment.

So Laurel wasn't the only one to be under the misapprehension that she had known Byron for some
considerable time?

'I went to all his games,' Kym said then. 'Even when
I was a little kid, Dad used to take me. We lived in
Adelaide, and a couple of times we went over to
Melbourne when he played for Carlton. It was great
having a famous footballer for a brother.' Kym paused.

'He shouldn't have given up the game, you know. He could have played on for years, even with his patched-up knee.' Kym frowned slightly, his eyes on the toes of his sneakers stretched out in front of him. 'He was the king pin at Carlton, and he could have named his price if he'd wanted to, and they'd have paid up. He was the club hero. No one mentions Aussie Rules without talking about Byron Willoughby. I reckon he was a fool to pack it in.'

'Perhaps he was tired of it,' Rebecca suggested. 'It must have taken up a lot of his time.'

'So what?' Kym retorted. 'It was his job just like any other job, except it was more exciting. He lost everything when he gave up playing football. He even broke his contract, and that cost him heaps of dollars.' Kym regarded her out of the corner of his eye, gauging her reaction. 'And then Nikki, his wife, ran off with his best friend.'

Rebecca's body tensed.

'She wasn't interested in a has-been football player,' he finished. 'And Byron's friend was Carlton's next best player.'

'That's hardly anything to do with me,' Rebecca told him. 'I'd say it was your brother's own business and I don't think we should discuss it.'

Kym gave a short laugh. 'We'd be the only ones who haven't talked about it. It was the hottest piece of gossip for ages. Famous footballer gives up the game. Famous footballer's beautiful wife leaves him to shack up with the player who took his place on the team. Famous footballer makes no comment. Even the kids at school were talking about it.'

Rebecca tried unsuccessfully to glean a clue to his feelings from his expression. Was that part of Kym's problem in his relationship with his brother? Did he think the idol he'd made of Byron had developed feet of clay? When all this had happened Kym would still have been at school. With the usual peer pressures and the media making the most of the whole affair, Kym might have been given a hard time.

Laurel had implied Byron's marriage hadn't been a happy one. Yet how much credence could she put on Kym's revelation about Nikki Willoughby?

'Well, it's all history now.' Rebecca made to change the subject.

'I guess so.' He was regarding her with that same open, assessing look she had disliked so much when she'd been introduced to him earlier. 'Now Byron has Bay Ridge and he's become a respectable "gentleman farmer", away from the bright lights and the crowd adoration of being a sports hero.' He paused slightly. 'And now he has you.'

Rebecca's head snapped around to stare at him, and to her horror she felt hot colour flood her face.

Kym smirked. 'You're not as beautiful as Nikki was, you know, but you're not bad-looking. Nikki was gorgeous, but kind of plastic, and she gushed all over everyone. You're much more, sort of, human.'

Rebecca's breath was caught in her chest. She wanted to stop this conversation, but she couldn't seem to utter a word.

'But then Byron always did have the knack of attracting neat-looking girls. They swarmed all over him,' Kym continued. 'Wow! It was mind-boggling. Wall-to-wall women.'

A coldness wrapped itself around Rebecca's heart. Hadn't she seen it all before, the way sportsmen were mobbed by female fans, much the way pop stars were? Hastily she blanked the picture from her mind.

'Look, Kym, you've got it all wrong,' she began, and his grin broadened into a knowing leer.

'It's OK, Rebecca. You don't have to explain to me. I'm just pleased Big Brother has made a better choice this time. Nikki gave Byron the run-around. She couldn't help it.' He shrugged. 'Every guy with eyes in his head fell all over her. But she didn't give a damn about anyone but herself. I don't think you're like that at all. You're a great improvement.'

Anger rose inside Rebecca, and she felt like a volcano about to erupt. She sat up tensely in her seat. Why, the supercilious little smart aleck deserved to be put over someone's knee.

'And by the way,' he was continuing, 'I know Laurel's a bit stuffy about things like this, but if you want to sleep with Byron, well, it's no sweat. We can change rooms after we go to bed. Laurel won't even know.'

CHAPTER SEVEN

FOR some moments Rebecca sat there stunned. How dared Kym even suggest such a thing? He was what? Seventeen? And he could sit there, barefaced and—— Words failed her.

'I don't mind, honestly,' he repeated, misconstruing Rebecca's silence.

'Well, I *do* mind,' she bit out angrily. 'And any swapping of rooms won't be necessary, thank you very much. Your brother is my employer—no more, no less. And I don't intend that you or anyone else should imply that our relationship is anything else, so you can stop all this understanding man-of-the-world dramatics as of right now.'

She paused for breath, and Kym held up his hands in a gesture of capitulation.

'OK. OK. You don't have to get uptight about it. I was only trying not to stand on any toes.' He shrugged. 'I just got the impression that you were Byron's woman—and——'

'I'm not Byron's woman,' Rebecca cut across him, speaking through clenched teeth. 'That's the most degrading, patronising expression you can use. Byron's woman. Good grief! That went out with the rest of the subjugative terms. Women do have a tentative hold on equal status these days, you know, if only on paper.' She looked him levelly in the eye. 'I'd advise you to take an honest look at yourself, Kym Willoughby, and decide whether you're going to remain a self-centred, condescending, egotistical little pain in the derrière, or whether you're going to grow up and become part of the human race, because I can't say much for your manners or up-bringing on current form.'

'Hey, come on. If I got things screwed up, I'm sorry.' He looked sulkily put out. 'But you can hardly blame me. I mean, I couldn't see Byron not making a pass at you at least. He'd have to be daft and blind.'

Rebecca bristled with anger, only spurred on by the fact that she knew she was blushing once more, and Kym held up his hands again.

'OK, I was wrong,' he said quickly. 'No need to fly off the handle. So I made a mistake. Let's just forget I ever mentioned it.'

Any retort Rebecca would have made was stifled as Laurel and Byron rejoined them. Although they both glanced sharply from Rebecca's set face to Kym's put-out frown, they made no comment, and Laurel silently passed them their drinks.

Rebecca drank her coffee quickly, intending to plead tiredness and escape to her room, but as she set down her empty cup Byron stood up.

'You haven't seen the view from the side patio,' he remarked easily, his gaze holding hers.

'I was going to slip up to bed,' she began.

'It will only take a minute.' He took her arm. 'Come on. It's especially lovely at night. Excuse us for a moment.'

Rebecca had no time to note anyone else's reaction to Byron's suggestion before he moved them down the path and around the corner of the house. What did he have in mind? Her senses clamoured again.

'Watch the step.'

They were on the raised patio now, standing side by side, and the township stretched below them, a myriad of lights in the darkness. Even in her agitation Rebecca expelled a sigh of wonder. 'It's beautiful.'

'Yes. Bill and Laurel have one of the best views in town. I thought you'd like to see it.' He leant on the patio rail beside her, and Rebecca slid a nervous sideways glance at him.

'What did Kym say to upset you?' he asked out of the blue, his tone evenly conversational.

'Kym?' Rebecca repeated uneasily.

'Yes. Kym, my brother,' Byron reiterated drily.

'What makes you think he upset me?'

'I could feel the vibes when Laurel and I rejoined you, and neither of you were exactly smiling. Apart from that, I've seen Kym at work before. He can be the rudest little upstart at times.'

Rebecca moved a few paces away from him. 'We had a difference of opinion, that's all. It was nothing earth-shattering.'

'What was it about?'

'Look, Byron, just forget it. It was between Kym and myself. I'm sorry I even mentioned it.'

'What did he say?'

Rebecca sighed. 'Can't we just leave it?'

'No, we can't.' His gaze locked with hers. 'Come on, Rebecca. Or should I go and ask my brother?'

'He just implied you and I were—well, more than friends,' she got out in a rush.

'And?'

'That's all.' Her eyes broke from his.

'You may as well finish it off.'

'He offered to swap rooms so we, you and I, could...'

There was a moment's heavy silence. 'That was most generous of him,' Byron said drily.

'Generous? It was damn presumptuous,' Rebecca got out, feeling her face colour. 'And I told him so, too.'

The shadow of a smile touched his lips. 'I'll bet you did,' he said softly, and when her chin lifted he shrugged. 'I'll talk to him, make him apologise.'

'There's no need. I've had my say and it's best forgotten. I don't think he'll make the same mistake again. And besides, I'd say that your getting in on the act would

only make it worse. If you tell him we aren't an item,'
Rebecca grimaced into the semi-darkness, 'then he'll
think we're protesting too much because it's true.'

'And that would never do,' Byron said softly, bringing
Rebecca's eyes around to look at him.

'No, it wouldn't, because it isn't true,' Rebecca replied, managing to keep her voice from deserting her.
'Far from it.'

'No.' The silence stretched between them then, began
to pull her unerringly towards him.

'I think,' Rebecca swallowed, 'I think we should go
back. I'm tired and I...'

'You want to go to bed,' he finished.

'Yes.' Rebecca moved off, down the couple of steps
to the path.

'No need to rush.' His hand clasped her elbow, slowing
her pace. 'You could turn your ankle. And, Becca,' he
added softly as they rounded the corner of the house,
'keep your door locked.' A faint hint of a smile touched
the corner of his mouth as they walked into the light
from the patio.

Lying alone in bed, Rebecca fumed over the situation.
Turning over, she punched her pillow into shape. Maybe
she was over-reacting. After all, there were plenty of girls
who would have jumped at the chance to move in with
a man like Byron. Perhaps she was just a prudish, old-
fashioned virgin. She smiled wryly at herself. Surely one
of the last left in captivity!

It was a casual, uninhibited world, so she was probably
being hard on Kym. He couldn't know she had set herself
her own standards that didn't include bed-hopping.

She sighed somewhat dejectedly. A small part of her
momentarily wished she was different, but she wasn't,
so that was the end of it.

Involuntarily, Byron's words returned to taunt her.
'Keep your door locked,' he'd said. Teasing her, surely?

Her eyes went in the direction of the closed door, and her thoughts progressed to the bedroom next door.

What would it be like to share his room, his bed, the closeness, the intimacy of his lovemaking? She could almost feel his hands on her body, his lips moving sensually on hers, the moulding of their naked flesh, arms and legs entwined, their quickened breathing.

Appalled at the trend of her thoughts, Rebecca suppressed the rising swell of her fast-beating heart. Her body felt hot and tense, and she shifted irritably. She would be best advised to put all thought of Byron Willoughby out of her mind and concentrate on getting to sleep. Nevertheless, with all her good intentions, she was awake long after she heard the others come upstairs to bed.

True to his word, the next morning Byron drove Rebecca down to the jetty to see if they could locate Rudy, and Tammy was thrilled to be going out with her father. She chattered happily from the moment they set out, and the presence of the child did blanket some of the tension that Rebecca knew lurked so close beneath the surface between Byron and herself.

Rebecca insisted he attend to his own business first, and when he returned he slid into the car and started the engine.

'I asked the clerk if he'd heard of Rudy Grainger working on a tuna boat,' he said as they headed away from the busy cargo office. 'He didn't know Rudy personally, but he thought he worked for Ray Vaughn on one of his boats. He made a phone call and came up with the *Blue Dancer*. As luck would have it, the *Blue Dancer* should be moored at the jetty now, so we may as well check it out.'

'Thank you.' Rebecca said softly. 'I hope he's here.' She glanced sideways at Byron, and their eyes met for a fraction of a second before he turned his attention back to the road.

'Who's Rudy?' Tammy's voice broke between them, and by the time Rebecca had explained to the little girl Byron had pulled the car into a parking place and the jetty activity swarmed around them.

The silos stood out starkly against the clear blue of the sky, and a long line of bulk grain trucks, tipping semi-trailers with high-sided aluminium bodies covered by green or blue tarpaulins, snaked across the dock area.

And there seemed to be people everywhere. Rebecca and Tammy looked about them, taking in all the constant activity.

'I'll just check that the *Blue Dancer* is still in port. I won't be long.'

Rebecca watched him stride away, tall and self-assured. He spoke to someone and they both turned in the direction of the length of the jetty before Byron nodded and came back towards the car. One of the truckies hailed him and he waved, laughing at the comment. A breath caught somewhere in Rebecca's chest. The sun shone on his dark hair, and he looked so incredibly handsome that he took her breath away.

With all the comings and goings milling around her, for that one earth-shattering moment only the two of them existed and everything else faded into the distance. I *am* in love with him, she acknowledged to herself, and a lump rose to catch painfully in her throat.

When she'd decided to return to Bay Ridge, she'd come in search of peace of mind, of a retrieved serenity. But love? Never love.

Byron rejoined them as Rebecca helped Tammy out of the car.

'We're in luck,' Byron was saying and Rebecca drew herself together with no little effort. He was watching her, but she dropped her gaze in case he saw her very raw feelings reflected there. 'We should find him on the boat.'

Wordlessly Rebecca nodded, and her eyes rose to follow his tall body as he strode around the car towards them. His dark hair glistening in the morning light was lifting in the sea breeze, and he moved with an easy masculine grace that set her heart beating in her breast like a trapped bird. Slowly Rebecca turned back to Tammy and took her hand.

Rudy was on board the tuna boat, and when he saw Rebecca his now bearded face broke into a wide smile of surprised pleasure as he vaulted up on to the jetty and swung her into his arms. Tears tumbled unchecked down Rebecca's cheeks as she turned her face into his shoulder.

'Hey, why the waterworks, Becca? Think of my reputation,' he teased her. 'Everyone will think I done you wrong or something. My sister,' he called out to some half-dozen or so interested deck-hands nearby, and there were loudly disbelieving guffaws.

Rebecca laughed, too, and dashed away the tears.

'I couldn't believe my eyes when I saw you and Will.' Rudy shot the other man a look and then raised his eyebrows. 'Hey, you two aren't together, are you? I mean, you know——'

'Of course not, Rudy,' Rebecca hastened to set Rudy straight.

'Oh.' Rudy's eyes went to Byron, and his expression clouded a little.

'How would you like to go along the jetty to see the grain ships loading up?' Byron asked his daughter flatly, taking Tammy's hand. With barely a glance at Rebecca, he left the two of them.

Rebecca's eyes followed him, and then she turned back to Rudy.

'What's between you two?' he asked.

'Nothing. I told you, I scarcely know him.' Rebecca forced a laugh. 'I want to talk about you. What on earth made you take up tuna fishing?'

'Why not? I had to do something, and I've always loved the sea; who wouldn't, growing up on an island?'

Rudy helped her down on to the deck and they sat in the shade of the cabin structure.

'I suppose you were shocked to hear Jock had sold the farm. I guess I'm to blame for that,' he said sheepishly. 'But I couldn't take it any more, Becca. I should have made the move years before. I'm just not a farmer. I never will be, and Jock had to see that.'

Rebecca nodded, knowing what he said was true.

Rudy told her he had a flat and, it seemed, a live-in girlfriend called Sandy whom he was planning to marry as soon as they'd saved enough money for the deposit on a house of their own. He assured her he'd never been happier.

'We're hoping to get married after this tuna season,' Rudy told her, and his smile faded a little. 'I'd really like to get married over on the island, Becca. Sandy hasn't any family, so how do you think Jock would feel about that? Do you think he'd come to the wedding?'

'Of course he would, Rudy,' Rebecca assured him. 'Jock knows why you left the farm and he understands. He's had time to cool down. Why don't you bring Sandy over for a visit some time so we can all get together? We should heal the old wounds.'

'He was pretty brassed off with me when I left. Wow! It was almost worse than the time he told you to marry Davie Kelly.'

Rebecca grimaced. 'And you didn't exactly back me up over that, either.'

'Davie wasn't so bad, Becca, and he always did have a thing about you.'

'Rubbish. He just liked girls. Davie Kelly had a roving eye.'

'Well, he liked what he saw of you, Becca.' Rudy grinned and then motioned along the jetty. 'So does Will, from what I saw.'

'Rudy, please. I've had it up to here,' Rebecca lifted her hand to her chin, 'with everyone implying that.'

Rudy's grin widened. 'He was the greatest Aussie Rules player of all time.' At the look on his sister's face he changed the subject. 'Are you over on holidays?'

'Not exactly. I was fed up with city life, and when Jock started writing more frequently I sort of decided to come home. I really needed the break, so I gave up my job, the flat, and came back to the island. I did get something of a shock when I discovered Bay Ridge didn't belong to Jock any more, though.'

And an even bigger shock when you turned out to be Byron Willoughby, she could have added.

'Jock didn't tell you when he wrote?'

Rebecca shook her head.

'I wonder why he didn't explain. Especially when he asked you to come home.'

'He didn't exactly ask me to come home,' Rebecca clarified. 'He just wrote more often.'

Rudy gave another guffaw of laughter. 'What's the betting Jock set it all up?'

'Set what up?' Rebecca frowned.

'Getting you and Will together.'

'Getting— Rudy!' Rebecca appealed to her brother, feeling colour wash her cheeks. It was one thing to think along those lines herself, but quite another to have Rudy voice it out loud.

'No, think about it, Becca. You know how fanatical Jock was about there always being Graingers on Bay Ridge. Well, if he married you off to Will he'd be ensuring the farm stayed in the family.'

'He wouldn't do that, Rudy,' Rebecca's tone wavered even as she denied her brother's supposition. She'd suspected it herself, after all, and it would explain such a lot. Jock's eagerness for her to get along with Byron, his insistence that she stay on to look after Tammy, and the out-of-character relaxation of his moral values. The

old Jock would never have left her alone in the house
with a man. Oh, Jock! The old leopard hadn't changed
his spots.

'Look, Rudy, I'm not interested in marriage. I'm
simply going to be working on Bay Ridge, looking after
Byron's daughter. I have to do something for my keep.'

Rudy winked audaciously.

'Rudy, for heaven's sake——'

'Just teasing, Becca.' He grinned. 'But even I have to
admit that Will's an improvement on Davie Kelly.'
Rebecca gave him a quelling look and he laughed. 'That's
the old Becca.' He sobered. 'It's good to see you again,
Sis. And don't worry. It'll all work out. Will's quite a
bloke.'

'I won't have anyone marrying me off, Rudy,' Rebecca
began, and Rudy held up his hand. 'Not before and not
now.'

'OK. I know. You're just working for him. Jock
should know better by now, shouldn't he?' Rudy
sobered. 'But I would like to make my peace with him,
Becca. Do you think you could set it up?'

'Of course.'

'Great.' He reached for his wallet and drew out a small
card. 'Here's Sandy's number. She's a hairdresser. You
can reach us at the salon where she works.'

They sat happily exchanging reminiscences.

'And did you notice much difference in the island?'
Rudy asked, and Rebecca shook her head.

'No, thankfully it seems unchanged. I half expected
progress to crawl all over it.'

'Give it time,' Rudy sympathised. 'Seen any of the
old crowd?'

Rebecca shook her head. 'Haven't really had time. I've
only been into Kingscote a couple of times.'

They stood up and leant on the ship's railing.

'I would have thought Davie Kelly would have been
on your doorstep the day after you arrived back. With

flowers, perhaps. And down on one knee.' Rudy gave a soft chuckle, but before Rebecca could chastise him a shadow fell across them and they both looked up on to the jetty.

Byron stood with Tammy beside him, his face set and unsmiling.

'We walked all the way to the end, and a man caught a bucketful of fish,' beamed the little girl.

'We should be getting back,' Byron said without preamble. 'Laurel may need the car.'

'Of course.' Rebecca scrambled up the short ladder with a good-natured boost from her brother. She smiled down at him from the jetty. 'I'll see you soon, Rudy.'

'Don't forget to put in a good word for me with Jock,' he called as they moved back along the jetty towards the car.

Tammy chattered away to her father and Rebecca, but Rebecca was only half listening to the little girl. She could feel the tension in the man beside her, and in the bright, warm sun she felt a shiver run up her spine.

Byron waited while Rebecca strapped his daughter into her seat-belt before walking around to open the passenger-side door for her.

'Who's Davie Kelly?' he asked softly, his words halting her move to step into the car.

CHAPTER EIGHT

'AN OLD flame?' Byron raised one dark brow.

'Not exactly,' Rebecca replied cautiously.

'Sounds like Mr Kelly is something of a knight errant.' He smiled, but his eyes bore in to Rebecca's. 'Flowers. Bended knee. Right out of a romantic novel.'

Rebecca's gaze locked with his, and although her lips parted she was unable to form a sarcastic reply. She should retort in kind but . . . he was far too close to her.

The bright sunlight lit his face, the tanned skin taut over firm jaw and cheekbones, that small scar, the now cold blue eyes, and his mouth. Her eyes touched on his lips and she couldn't draw her gaze away. She was held spellbound. She'd never wanted to be kissed more than she did at that moment.

Neither of them moved.

'Daddy. Becca.' Tammy's voice seemed to slice between them, sever the explosive bond that held them, fused them together. 'Look, Rudy's waving goodbye to us.'

The massive engine of the vehicular ferry, *Troubridge*, vibrated gently beneath their feet as Byron led them to the upper deck so that Tammy could see the night-lights of Port Lincoln. The jetty jutted out into the bay to their right, and the ferry was berthed stern-first so that the cars, caravans, trailers, etc. could be driven aboard.

Byron had spent the afternoon fishing from the Korton Point jetty with Bill and the children, leaving Laurel and Rebecca to rest at home. Kym was farewelling his cronies, returning to his sister's house with barely time to collect

117

his gear before they left to board the ferry. Both Byron and Laurel took him to task for his lateness.

Now he was leaning disgruntledly over the rail as Byron lifted Tammy up so she could get a better view of the lights and the activity on the jetty below them. The breeze was fresh, but nowhere near as strong as it had been the day Rebecca returned to Kangaroo Island from Adelaide, and she brushed a few tendrils of dark curls back from her face as a gust of wind caught at her hair. Of course, as far as the weather went, here in the shelter of the bay could be no indication of conditions out in the open sea.

After those tense moments by Laurel's car Byron had all but ignored Rebecca's presence, only speaking to her when he had to, and she felt limp and listless, her muscles weak with the aftermath of that short, volatile encounter.

If Rebecca hadn't known better she would have said Byron was jealous. He showed all the classic signs. Who was Davie Kelly? Rebecca could almost laugh. Davie Kelly meant nothing to her. If Byron but knew it, every man she had ever met paled into insignificance compared to himself.

They had made their farewells and could see Laurel, Bill and the children on the dock below them.

'Everyone's so small, they look like the people of Lilliput,' Tammy exclaimed, waving enthusiastically at her cousins. 'Isn't it high up here, Becca? I bet even Daddy looks small.'

'Impossible, Tammy,' Kym muttered sulkily, and Byron turned away in exasperation.

'We'll be leaving in a few minutes,' he said evenly. 'Let's go below and settle down for the night.'

Luckily there were relatively few other passengers in the forward lounge, so they could spread out for a more comfortable night if they so wished. The seats were only semi-recliners, so they put two large cushions on the floor for Tammy and tucked a blanket around her. Although she was excited about the trip, she was tired, and by the time they were under way her eyelids were drooping.

Byron saw them settled and then left them to go below to talk to one of their neighbours who was making the trip back to the island with some new stock. Kym threw his legs over the arm of a chair and began leafing boredly through a magazine. With a sigh Rebecca stretched out, half sitting up in the seat behind Tammy, trying to sleep. She was tired, too.

Since the evening before, when she had told Kym off, they had barely spoken to each other and Kym had been careful not to find himself alone with her. And now, so it seemed, had his brother.

That was fine by Rebecca. If they were to co-exist in such close proximity, then that was the way they would have to keep it. Light and detached. Uncomplicated and unemotional. Especially where Byron was concerned, Rebecca grimaced to herself. But that was so much easier said than done. To accomplish that, she had to keep her distance from him. When she was close to him, her good intentions scattered like leaves in the wind around Cape du Couedic. Their encounter this morning had proved that to her.

And as she sat there, churning inside, she wished, no matter how much effort she put into quelling the feeling, that things could be different. If only she could have met Byron Willoughby somewhere else, at some other time, without the complications of Bay Ridge, and the feelings he still nurtured for his beautiful, if unfaithful, wife. The confused emotions that tumbled inside her reminded her that an involvement with a man like Byron Willoughby would be pure folly.

The steward had switched out the main lights in the cabin, and only the dull glow of a night-light lit the lounge. Most of the other passengers had settled down, but Byron still hadn't returned.

Rebecca stifled a yawn. She was physically tired but mentally alert. Her mind kept turning everything over and always came back to Byron Willoughby. Resolutely, she put him firmly from her thoughts and tried to sleep.

The ferry rose on a swell, and Rebecca automatically braced herself. She found herself remembering her first meeting with Byron, and she grimaced. One case of mistaken identity, a kiss shared with a total stranger, and now her whole even-keeled world was totally upturned. She squeezed her eyes closed, and Byron's face, dark and rugged, filled her mind's eye to the exclusion of all else.

She slept eventually, only to stir drowsily as Byron slid into the seat beside her.

'Tammy?' she murmured, only half awake.

'She's fine,' Byron assured her softly. 'I'll keep an eye on her. Get some sleep while you can, Becca; we're heading for a rough trip, according to the captain.'

Byron's breath teased the hair at her temple and she let herself relax, not totally taking in his words, and her head fell sideways on to his shoulder.

Some part of her knew it was a mistake to be so close to him, warned her it was, but she couldn't wake herself up enough to listen. Especially if Rudy was right. If Jock had set up this meeting between her and Byron—— But he couldn't have. It was ridiculous and she wouldn't even consider it. Still, she should move away from him. But she was so wonderfully warm, and his shoulder was so comfortable. And she could even believe she felt the feather-soft touch of his lips against her temple. It was a lovely dream.

Rebecca's first indication that the weather had deteriorated came when she was thrown sideways, the movement waking her with rude suddenness. Her eyes swung to the seat beside her, but Byron had gone. She stood up, clutching the back of the seat in front of her for support as Byron appeared with a fretful Tammy in his arms.

He sat down, holding the little girl on his knee, and Rebecca sank into the chair beside him. Tammy's eyes were large in her small, pale face.

'I don't like this boat, Daddy. I don't feel very good,' she whimpered, and by the time they'd reached the more turbulent waters of a group of reefs known as the Althorpes, a notorious section of converging currents off the end of York Peninsula, she had been horribly sick.

The *Troubridge* forged sturdily onwards, but the pitching of the boat made sleeping for the adults virtually impossible. In her father's arms Tammy dozed fitfully, but Rebecca was never more pleased to feel the change in the ship's movements that heralded the shelter of the island's land mass.

She relaxed a little, and Byron returned the now sleeping Tammy to her makeshift bed. Rebecca slept again too, and the rosy light of dawn was rolling over the wide expanse of ocean when the sound of the steward lifting the mesh shutters on the café woke her. She sat up and flexed her stiff muscles.

'Morning.' Byron slid into his seat beside her. He looked bright and vital, showing no sign of his disturbed night. 'Would you like some breakfast?'

'Mmm.' Rebecca stretched again, her gaze falling from his as his eyes swept over the swell of her breasts outlined beneath her pale windcheater.

'What time is it?' she asked breathily.

'Breakfast time.' He smiled, and Rebecca smiled automatically back at him.

Their eyes met and held again, passing that same silent, sensual message, and Rebecca forced her rubbery legs to stand up.

'I think I'll freshen up, too.' She picked up her bag and stepped past him to see that Tammy was also stirring.

Although she was still pale, the little girl seemed to be over the worst of her bout of seasickness.

She took Tammy with her and they had a quick wash and cleaned their teeth. Rebecca brushed her own hair and then attended to Tammy's, straightening the little girl's pink, fleecy tracksuit.

'Will we be there soon?' Tammy asked as they rejoined Byron and Kym.

'In half an hour or so,' her father told her.

He had tea and a snack waiting for them, and Tammy smiled shakily as Byron encouraged her to eat a piece of toast.

'This is just like a picnic, isn't it?' She sighed theatrically. 'I'm sorry I was sick last night, but the boat wouldn't stay still.'

Byron gave her a hug and kissed the tip of her nose. 'No worries, chicken.'

'I don't think I like being on boats as much as I like looking at them,' she said sadly.

They went up on deck to watch the shape of Kangaroo Island get steadily closer, and Byron pointed out the landmarks to Tammy. Kym was silent, although he didn't seem to have suffered the pangs of seasickness that Tammy had.

The *Troubridge* docked stern-first at the jetty at Kingscote, and Rebecca was amazed again at the precision handling of the large boat as it was manoeuvred into its berth with only inches to spare. Even this early there was quite a bit of movement on the jetty that jutted into Nepean Bay.

A few people strolled along to watch the unloading, and a couple of stalwart fishermen had cast their lines hopefully into the water but didn't seem to be catching anything. Rebecca couldn't imagine any sensible fish being within a mile of the jetty, with the noise of the prime-movers rumbling over the planking.

Jock was there with Byron's Commodore to pick them up, and Tammy gave him a big hug. He shook his head sympathetically when she told him all about her ordeal. The little girl was tired and fretful, so once they arrived home Rebecca put her straight to bed.

The adults sat around the kitchen table drinking tea, and Jock filled Byron in on the progress they'd made while he was away. Eventually the men decided to inspect the west paddock, and with a sideways look at Rebecca Kym chose to accompany them, the three of them driving off in Jock's utility.

Tammy woke up before lunch, and Rebecca then spent the afternoon with her, fixing up Rudy's old bedroom opposite her own for the little girl. They packed what was left of Rudy's things into a trunk, and shifted the furniture around until Tammy was satisfied everything was to her liking. She set her favourite teddy bear on the bed and then helped Rebecca stow away her clothes in the wardrobe and chest of drawers.

'Aunt Laurel packed all my toys in a big box, and Daddy will bring them back with him when he goes down to the jetty later,' she told Rebecca. 'Wait till you see them all, Becca. I can put my doll's house right here on this little table.' She sighed happily. 'It's going to be such fun being here with Daddy and you. Oh, and Jock and Kym.'

During the first week of the school break, Rebecca and Tammy were left to their own devices. Rebecca was amazed at how easy it was to be with the little girl all day.

Tammy had a bright and sunny nature, and she was happy to follow Rebecca around. She helped Rebecca spring clean the house, and sat excitedly beside her when she drove into Kingscote to pick up their groceries.

The little girl chatted all the while, and Rebecca could see none of the insecurity that Laurel had warned her about. Yet Tammy never once mentioned her mother.

It was as though her life had commenced with her stay with Laurel. When they'd unpacked Tammy's toys, she proudly showed Rebecca a framed photograph of her father in his football uniform, his Brownlow Medal around his neck.

'Daddy's a very famous footballer,' she solemnly told Rebecca as she carefully lifted the photo out of the box. 'He can jump so high, higher than anybody, to catch the ball.'

The photo had pride of place on the little girl's dressing-table, and each time Rebecca entered the room her own eyes were drawn to that handsome, laughing face.

Of Byron and Kym they saw little, for they were busy from daylight until dusk working out in the west paddock, to return tired and hungry at dinner-time. So much for Byron's assuring Laurel he would be spending more time with his daughter, Rebecca reflected irritably as she heard Tammy giggling while Byron tucked her into bed for the night. After his high-handed bossiness at dinner, which she meant to tackle him about later, she was in no mood to listen to the obvious amusement he was sharing with his daughter.

She returned to the dining-room where Jock and Kym were finishing their coffee and began collecting the empty cups.

'We can do that, love,' insisted Jock, taking the cups from her. 'Bring those through, lad,' he directed Kym.

Kym picked up his cup and it slipped out of his fingers, to smash loudly on the floor.

'Oh, hell!' he swore as he bent down to collect up the pieces.

Rebecca helped him, and they were just getting to their feet when Byron came in.

'What was that?' he asked, his eyes going from Rebecca to his brother.

'I just dropped a cup, that's all,' Kym stated defensively. 'You can deduct it from my wages.'

'We've picked up all the pieces,' Rebecca put in quickly, levelly holding Byron's gaze.

His set expression told her he still hadn't forgotten their brief argument at dinner either.

'Well, you're a bit of a failure at waitressing,' Jock teased Kym, lightening the tense atmosphere. 'What are you like at cooking, lad?'

'Not as good as Rebecca,' he replied, relaxing a little, but his eyes went from his brother to Rebecca, quietly assessing.

When he caught Rebecca's eye his gaze fell away, but Rebecca was aware of the direction of his thoughts. She sensed he still believed she was having an affair with his brother.

With everything cleared away, Jock retired to his cottage while Kym, as was usual, went to his room, Jock's old bedroom at the back of the house, to listen to his stereo.

Resolutely Rebecca sought Byron out. She had no intention of leaving their argument unfinished. He was in the living-room, sitting in his chair, his feet crossed on the coffee table, reading the newspaper.

'Could I see you for a few moments?' she asked, walking a couple of tentative paces into the room.

Byron looked up and folded the newspaper, dropping it onto his lap. 'Sure. Come and sit down.'

Rebecca preferred to stand. 'It's about our trip over to Stokes Bay,' she began.

'Mmm.' Byron's eyes were regarding her, and a shiver slid down her spine.

She took another step forward to conceal the involuntary movement. 'Well, as I said at dinner, I don't see any reason why I can't drive over there myself.'

He raised his eyebrows arrogantly.

'Good grief! It's not far, and I could just about drive there in my sleep.'

He put his feet on the floor and straightened in his chair, tossing the folded newspaper on to the coffee-table.

'I thought we'd decided all this at dinner,' he commented expressionlessly.

Rebecca's dark eyes clashed stormily with his, and only the heavy ticking of the grandfather clock cut into the silence. 'You decided, you mean.'

'All right. I decided, then,' he agreed calmly, and his composure only served to inflame Rebecca's anger.

'For heaven's sake, I'm sorry I even mentioned I intended taking Tammy swimming. The rock pool's quite safe and there's shade from the sun, besides the beach umbrella I was going to take with us. So there's no need for you to drag yourself away from your work, is there? I know how busy you are,' she finished drily, and then could have bitten her tongue at the tone she'd used.

Byron raised his head. 'Do I sense a mild rebuke there?' he asked evenly.

'Take it as you like.' Rebecca refused to back down, even though her heartbeats fluttered erratically.

'Would you care to explain?'

'You haven't exactly seen much of your daughter since she came here.'

He frowned. 'Has Tammy been upset about that?'

'Well, no. Not exactly. But she hasn't been used to seeing much of you. However, you did tell Laurel you'd be spending some time with her.' As soon as the words were out Rebecca knew she'd played right into his hands.

'Which is why I decided to come with you to Stokes Bay tomorrow afternoon.' He smiled self-satisfiedly. 'I wonder if Laurel realised that you'd carry on where she left off. Very conscientious of you, Becca.' He laughed then in genuine amusement before sobering. 'Seriously, Becca, I do appreciate what you're doing with my daughter. She likes you and she enjoys being with you.'

'Well——' Rebecca's anger subsided '—thank you, but I *am* only filling in temporarily until you find someone permanent,' she reminded him. 'And if you'd like to spend the afternoon with Tammy tomorrow, then I could stay here and give you some time alone with her.'

'Don't be ridiculous.' He frowned irritatedly. 'Of course you're coming, too. I thought you told Jock you were looking forward to seeing the bay again.'

Rebecca's eyelashes fell to shield the expression in her eyes. She had been. But to be going with him—was she looking forward to that? If she was honest, she'd have to admit she was. But she couldn't let him know that, nor that being virtually alone with him made her afraid. Not of him, but of herself. Did he realise that?

'Aren't you looking forward to revisiting old childhood haunts?' He smiled again. 'I'll be back here before lunch, so we can take a picnic with us to eat on the beach. Tammy will love that.'

He was so very sure of himself. And of her, it seemed. Rebecca felt her anger flare up again.

'If you must know, I didn't appreciate having the plans made in front of everyone. You could have had the decency to mention it to me privately, so that I wasn't just hit with it in front of Kym.'

'What's Kym got to do with it?' His brows drew together.

'I didn't like being taken by surprise, that's all.' How could she tell him that Kym's knowing look had disconcerted her and resulted in her anger? Kym obviously thought Byron was using the trip to Stokes Bay as an excuse to be with her, especially when Byron refused Kym's suggestion that he have the afternoon off as well and accompany them to the beach, too.

'I didn't want Kym along, as it would leave Jock short-handed. Kym's the main reason why I've been unable to spend time with Tammy.' He ran a hand through his dark hair. 'You've noticed my relationship with my young brother isn't exactly full of sweetness and light. It was the same before I left Melbourne. I'd planned to wait and see if Kym was prepared to work on the farm before I committed myself to leaving him with Jock. Jock's not a young man, and I wouldn't expect to drop everything on him before I'd seen for myself that Kym was going to pull his weight.'

Rebecca felt herself weakening, her anger simmering down.

'But, all that aside,' he continued edgily, 'it was hardly anything to do with Kym, was it?'

When Rebecca paused before replying, he stepped towards her. 'What is all this between you and Kym? Has he been bothering you again?'

'Of course not,' Rebecca denied hotly.

'If I thought he'd touched you, Becca——'

'Touched me?' she repeated incredulously. 'He's just a boy. How could you think that?'

'Believe me, Kym's hardly a boy. And he's not blind, you know. You're a beautiful girl who's here and available.'

'Available?' Rebecca gave a snicker of disbelief. 'What exactly do you mean by available?'

'I mean, unattached.'

'And obviously so frustrated I'd take any offers, even from an adolescent boy years younger than myself?'

'That's not what I meant.'

Rebecca's hands went to her hips. 'It sure sounded like that from this side of the room.'

'I meant that young boys of seventeen are——'

'Spare me a lecture about the birds and the bees, Byron. You aren't my father, you know.'

His lips thinned. 'Oh, I do know that, Becca, believe me. And if you want it plainly, then here it is.' He stepped closer, so that now she could have lifted a hand to touch him, and she had to tip her head back to meet his stormy gaze. 'I don't know what sort of life you led in Sydney.

Maybe you're used to having,' he paused, 'someone around.'

Rebecca couldn't believe what she was hearing, and she flushed at his implication.

'You didn't exactly fend me off,' he continued, 'so perhaps you didn't discourage Kym.'

'How dare you even suggest...suggest...' Rebecca's hand swung upwards, but his reflexes were a match for her. He effortlessly captured her hand before the blow made contact, and with one precise twist of his wrist she was brought up against him.

For seemingly endless seconds they stood together, bodies in contact, and then just as suddenly he released her, broken them apart.

'Don't ever do that again, Becca. You may not care for the consequences.'

'Oh! And what might these consequences be?'

'Becca,' he warned quietly, but she was beyond caution.

'Well? Since you think you can come the autocratic father with me, I guess you'll ground me for a week as punishment.' Rebecca folded her arms and smiled mockingly up at him.

Byron shook his head. 'Oh, no, Becca. You're not going to goad me any more tonight.'

'But grounding me would rebound on you, too, wouldn't it?' Rebecca continued as though he hadn't spoken. 'I wouldn't be available for the dance we're all to attend on Friday night, would I?'

Not long after their argument about the Stokes Bay trip, Kym had mentioned the football club dance and Byron had implied they were all going, much to Tammy's delight.

'I don't suppose it occurred to you that I may not want to go to this dance?' she threw at him.

'Jock told me you used to enjoy the local dances. I've been coaching the local team, so Jock and I generally go. Everyone will expect us to be there as usual.' He turned to pick up his newspaper.

'And so I'm expected to go along, too?' Rebecca asked, lifting her chin, her anger rising at his calm dismissal.

Byron gave an irritated sigh, dropping the newspaper back on to the coffee-table before turning to face her. 'No, not *expected* to go along,' he bit out. 'We'll all be going. The whole family. Jock, Kym, you, me and Tammy.'

'Oh, I see. You want a babysitter,' she challenged him, realising she was behaving badly, but unable to stop herself.

'No, I don't want a damn babysitter,' Byron expelled an exasperated breath, raising his hands and letting them fall in obvious annoyance. 'Look, what's wrong with coming to the dance with us? Why make such an issue of it?'

'If I'm not the babysitter, what am I—the great Byron Willoughby's latest woman?' The words came bitterly from Rebecca's lips before she was even aware she was thinking them, and now it was too late to draw them back. She took a step away from him in absolute horror. Why had she said that?

Byron's head went up, his eyes narrowing, and he was in front of her, mere inches from her, in two long strides, his fingers reaching out to close around her wrist.

'I——' Rebecca gulped, her voice failing her, her heart hammering in her ears. 'I'm sorry.' She swallowed again. 'I shouldn't have——'

'No. You shouldn't,' he agreed with menacing quietness.

CHAPTER NINE

SHE mustn't let him intimidate her, Rebecca told herself, and drew herself determinedly together. 'Well, it's only what everyone thinks,' she put in defiantly.

'Everyone?' He coldly raised one dark eyebrow. 'Who's everyone?'

'Laurel. Kym,' Rebecca stammered.

'I wasn't aware that my sister or my young brother took such an avid interest in my love-life, or lack of it.' He smiled, the humour not reaching the dark blue pools of his eyes. 'So both Kym and Laurel think you and I have got something going. I wonder what gave them that idea? Or should I say who?'

Rebecca's anger overcame her apprehension as she tried unsuccessfully to twist her hand from his hold. 'Why, you conceited, self-opinionated—— If you think I gave them any reason to suspect a thing, then you're very much mistaken. You're the one who insisted I accompany you to Port Lincoln in the first place.'

'And I was under the impression that I explained why I did,' he said, just as angrily. 'But we still haven't sorted out this,' he paused, 'interesting misconception.'

'Oh, forget it!' Rebecca snapped. 'Now let me go.' She pulled against his hold. 'I want to go to bed. You and I know it's not true, so there's no point in going over it again.'

His glittering gaze bore down into her, left her widening eyes to touch on the slight tremble of her lips, and she caught her breath, the tip of her tongue nervously moistening their sudden dryness.

'Do we, Becca?' he asked softly.

131

'Do we . . . what?' Her own voice was huskily thick.

'Know it's not true, that there's nothing between us?'

Her eyes were now enmeshed, locked on the sensual curve of his lips, and, this close, the dusky shadow on his chin and jaw were pinpricks of tiny, individual dark hairs.

'Of course,' she said, the words barely a whisper. 'Of course we do,' she repeated, a little louder this time as she fought to put some conviction into her voice.

Byron laughed softly, deep in his chest, a profoundly sensuous sound that rang warning bells loudly in Rebecca's mind. 'Of course we don't,' he said, and his hand exerted only the slightest pressure on her wrist to draw her forward those few precious separating inches to bring their bodies together.

He lowered his head and his lips touched, feather-soft, on hers, gently caressing first her top lip, then her bottom lip, sliding along her jawline to her sensitive earlobe, teasing her nerve-endings until a sharp, involuntary shiver had her trembling against him.

'No,' she gulped out the word and the warm breath of his 'yes' against her ear only further inflamed the growing glow of her aching need.

An uncontrollable yearning was rising within her, insisting on being given free rein. Rebecca turned her head to ward him off, but his lips easily found hers and his gentle caress deepened, his tongue-tip spearing barbs of desire that exploded inside her, shooting her control down in flames.

Her lips parted and her body moved pliantly against him. Her hands were resting against his chest, her fingers curling into the soft cotton of his shirt, while his hands cupped the back of her head, his fingers twining in the dark softness of her hair. He moved his hips against her, and the realisation of the extent of his arousal sent the blood pounding through her veins.

Dear God! She wanted him as much as he so obviously wanted her. Until she'd met him she'd been totally unaware of the depth of passion lying dormant inside her. Byron had awoken her. And she exulted in it, wanted to throw her previous ideals to the four winds, wanted only this moment with Byron to go on for ever.

His body was locked against her, moulded to her arching contours. When his lips surrendered hers, the sound of their ragged breathing filled the room. His hands were still holding her head and he gazed down at her, his arousal tempering the hard planes of his cheekbones and jaw, softening the firm line of his mouth, and his long, dark lashes fell to shield the burning blaze in his eyes.

'Of course we don't,' he repeated huskily, with an edge of self-derisive mockery.

He released her then and stepped back from her, leaving her standing alone, and the sudden withdrawal of the heat of his body was like a cold, icy gust of wind enveloping her. She felt rejected. Her gaze held his, but she was unable to read his shuttered expression.

'And God knows what I'm going to do about it,' he muttered half to himself, raking an impatient, still slightly unsteady hand through his hair again.

Rebecca's eyes dropped downwards over the tautness of his body, over his chest, the flat stomach, the tensed thighs making it obvious that he was still aroused, and her heartbeats caught painfully in her chest. He still wanted her and yet he'd pushed her away from him. She drew her eyes from him, feeling hot colour flood her cheeks.

'You'd better go, Becca,' he said tiredly, and her eyes flashed up to meet his.

He was dismissing her again. The situation had got a little too carried away for his liking. Perhaps her unrestrained response had put him off. Or maybe he liked to make the running. And now he was telling her to go.

Humiliation rose within her like bile. How could he? What kind of man was he, that he could turn his emotions on and off like a tap? Well, he wasn't going to get away with it.

'Now that you've finished with me, you mean?' she tossed at him angrily.

He had started to swing away from her, but he froze momentarily at her words before turning slowly back to face her.

'Rebecca.' He said her name warningly, but she ignored his admonition.

'And if I choose not to—go—as you put it?' She lifted her head mutinously.

'Rebecca, don't push it.'

'Don't push what? You? I wouldn't think of it. The great Byron Willoughby has to call all the shots, doesn't he?' Her eyes flashed over him as her voice rose. 'We wouldn't want to upset him by not following his every direction. Oh, no, when Byron Willoughby says jump, we all have to say, how high, sir?'

He reached her in a stride, his hands clasping her upper arms, dragging her cruelly against him so that the breath was almost knocked from her body. His mouth claimed hers, his lips crushing, punishing, so that she whimpered deep in her throat. He bent her backwards so that her hands clutched at his arms for support, and hot tears filled her eyes.

Then, just as suddenly, she was free. He glared down at her, his face dark and thunderous, totally the dominant male.

Rebecca blinked back her tears and wiped her mouth with the back of her hand. He saw her bruised lips, and she heard him draw a sharp breath.

'Becca——' he began, his hand reaching out towards her, but she slapped it away.

'Don't touch me!' she cried angrily. 'Don't you touch me again.'

'Touch you?' His own anger rekindled. 'I should——'

'Daddy. Becca.' Tammy's tearful voice halted Byron in mid-sentence, and they both turned to face the little girl hovering uncertainly in the doorway.

'What's the matter? Why are you fighting?' Two large tears ran down her cheeks. 'I don't want you to fight,' she sobbed, and threw herself at her father.

Byron lifted her into his arms, soothing her gently, and over Tammy's dark head his eyes met Rebecca's and then fell.

Rebecca was horrified and ashamed. She wished the floor would open up and swallow her. Absorbed in herself, she had completely forgotten Tammy was only a room away. And now the little girl was upset. Rebecca moved forward and ran a hand over Tammy's tousled head.

'Tammy, don't cry,' she said softly. 'It's all right.'

Tammy lifted her head from Byron's shoulder. 'But you and Daddy were fighting, and I don't want you to go away, Becca. I don't.'

'I'm not going away,' Rebecca assured her.

'Mummy did. Daddy rowed with her and she went away.' Tammy's sobs recommenced.

Helplessly, Rebecca's gaze found Byron's, but his expression was as inscrutable as ever.

'Becca's not leaving,' he said gently. 'We were just discussing something and we both got a bit loud, that's all, Tammy.' He lifted her chin and smiled reassuringly down at her. 'Come on now, no more tears. You should be fast asleep. I'll come and tuck you in again.'

'Becca, too?' she asked, sniffing somewhat forlornly, and Byron nodded.

Rebecca followed them through to Tammy's room, crossing to straighten the bedclothes before Byron deposited his daughter in the bed. He gave her a hug and kissed her on the nose.

'Sleep tight, and I'll see you in the morning.'

Tammy nodded and turned to hold her arms out to Rebecca. As her arms slid around Rebecca's neck, she whispered loudly, 'Shall I ask Daddy to promise not to growl at you again?'

Rebecca laughed and hugged her tightly.

'I don't think he would growl at Becca if she was as good as you are.' Byron's wry voice came from behind Rebecca, and she didn't look at him as she made a big job of tucking in the blankets.

Tammy giggled. 'You mustn't misbehave, Becca,' she scolded.

Rebecca pulled a teasing face at her. 'No, I mustn't, must I?'

'Becca.' Tammy's hand held tightly to Rebecca's. 'Becca, you won't leave, will you? Promise?'

'No, I won't.' Rebecca squeezed the little girl's hand.

'Cross your heart?' Tammy's large eyes pleaded.

'Cross my heart. OK?'

Tammy nodded solemnly and Rebecca kissed her goodnight. Straightening, she murmured a goodnight in Byron's general direction, her eyes not meeting his, before she made a quick exit to her room.

She went straight to bed, although she wasn't in the least tired. She was far too high to sleep, way up on a soaring plane, on to which Byron's lovemaking had lifted her. Even their bitter argument afterwards had not brought her back to earth.

Her body was vibrantly alive, still tingling, throbbing from his touch.

It was her own fault, she told herself. She had purposefully goaded him. She'd known she was doing it, but she'd been unable to stop herself. Some demon had driven her. And, in his pent-up wrath at her incitement, Byron had angrily retaliated.

Her fingers rubbed the flesh of her upper arms where his fingers had grasped her, bruising with the force of

his hold on her. She would bear the marks tomorrow.
She shivered slightly. And yet, in their reciprocated anger,
they had been unable to disguise their mutual desire for
each other. And she still ached for him.

For what seemed like hours, Rebecca lay there, unable
to find the peaceful oblivion of sleep. She kept on tossing
everything over in her mind. Byron. Tammy. The im-
plications of the child's feelings of insecurity. They had
started with the loss of her mother, and continued with
her separation from her father. And, if Rebecca stayed
on at Bay Ridge, Tammy would become even more at-
tached to her, so that when the time came for Rebecca
to leave, then more damage would be done to a child
already emotionally disturbed.

Rebecca had just turned over for what seemed like the
hundredth time, when Tammy's cry of terror had her
out of bed and across the room to wrench open the door
before the sound of the child's cries had died away. She
flew across the hall and flicked on the light in Tammy's
room, hurrying over to the bed.

Tammy was sitting up, crying, and fear filled her eyes
as she blinked up at Rebecca.

'What's the matter, love?' Rebecca gathered her in to
her arms.

'I had a bad dream,' Tammy wept, her arms so tightly
wrapped around Rebecca's neck that she was almost
strangling her.

'Don't cry,' Rebecca soothed. 'It's all right now.'

'What's going on?' Kym appeared in the doorway.

'She woke up with a fright,' Rebecca told him softly.

'Gee! I nearly had a heart attack. I was in the kitchen
getting a drink. Frightened the life out of me. Was it
another of her nightmares?' Kym stood aside as Byron
appeared behind him.

As he crossed to the bed, his hair tousled, he was still
knotting the belt of his robe, the lapels falling slightly
open to reveal the dark mat of hair on his chest. His

face looked a little drawn, and he had obviously been woken from a deep sleep. Beneath the short robe Byron's legs were bare, and hastily Rebecca drew her eyes away from him.

'It was a bad dream, Daddy. A scary one.' Tammy turned into her father's arms, and Rebecca slowly stood up.

'Would you like a drink of water, Tammy?' she asked, and the little girl nodded sleepily, not slackening her hold on her father.

Kym moved from the doorway to let her past him, and she saw him looking across the hall through the open door of her room, taking in the single bed, the tumble of bedclothes where Rebecca had thrown aside the blankets when she ran into Tammy's room. When she turned from the tap with Tammy's glass of water, she was surprised to see Kym had followed her into the kitchen.

'Will she be all right?' he asked, the movement of his head indicating the direction of Tammy's bedroom.

'Yes. As soon as she gets back to sleep. I think most children occasionally have bad dreams.'

He nodded thoughtfully. 'I reckon I remember having a few in my time.'

Rebecca smiled faintly. 'Me, too.'

A cold draught came through the partially open kitchen window and she shivered, suddenly aware that she hadn't stopped to put on her robe. The clinging material of her nightdress, although it wasn't in the least transparent, moulded her shape like a second skin. She moved forward to pass Kym, but as she did so he spoke her name.

'Rebecca, I—umm—I'd like to apologise.'

She stopped to stare at him in surprise, sensing he didn't often find the necessity to do so.

'Apologise? For what?' she asked.

'For giving you a hard time and for not really believing you.'

Rebecca frowned.

'Well, not exactly for not believing you, but I thought there was no way you and Byron weren't—well, you know.' He made a helpless gesture with his hands.

'No, I don't know,' Rebecca declared.

'You see, I just saw your bed, in your room, and I realised you weren't with Byron and I— I thought Byron put me out in the back room so I'd be out of the way, so you two could... Heck, Becca, I'm sorry,' he finished lamely.

'Oh, Kym, I told you before how things were between your brother and myself,' she began firmly.

He looked like an overgrown schoolboy standing there in his pyjamas, his hair uncombed, and Rebecca found herself laughing softly.

She shook her head. 'OK. Apology accepted,' she told him. 'And let it be a lesson to you, Kym Willoughby, not to jump to conclusions without any firm evidence to back them up.'

'Right.' He grinned at her, and she decided again that he could be quite likeable, that there might be some hope for him yet.

'If you think Tammy'll be OK I'll go back to bed,' he said.

'I think she will. Byron should have settled her down now. She'll probably sleep the rest of the night through undisturbed.' Rebecca stifled a yawn. 'At least, I hope so.'

'Me, too.' His eyes ran over her body clad in the clinging nightdress, and then rose to meet her gaze. He reached out and touched her arm, leaning forward to plant a quick kiss on her cheek. 'Big Brother sure is letting the grass grow under his feet. He needs his head read.' He laughed a little self-consciously and walked off down the hall to his room. 'Maybe I should have a nightmare, too,' he added, slanting a quick glance back over his shoulder at Rebecca before he disappeared.

Rebecca stood holding the glass of water and groaned softly. Perhaps it would have been better for things to have stayed the way they were. Byron's words returned to her. "Kym's hardly a boy. And he's not blind... You're a beautiful girl who's here and available."

Kym's assessing look had been anything but boyish. She rubbed her hands tiredly over her eyes. Not more complications, surely?

She made herself move to return to Tammy's room, only to find that the little girl was already almost asleep. Byron had pulled up a chair to sit by the bed, and he had switched off the main light, leaving only the soft glow of the bedside lamp burning. She walked quietly across to set the glass of water on the dresser.

'She's all right now,' Byron said. 'You go to bed. I'll stay with her until she settles.'

'Are you sure?' Rebecca whispered. His face looked a little drawn and tired.

Byron nodded, and she saw his eyes fall the length of her body, the way Kym's had done in the kitchen just a moment ago. Only this time her heartbeats accelerated wildly, a burning heat rising inside her. Hastily she turned away to pause in the doorway, facing him again. And his eyes still watched her. To Rebecca they appeared to gleam brightly in the half-light. How she wanted to run to him...

'I'll leave my door open in case she stirs after you've gone to bed,' she said a little breathily. 'Goodnight.'

'Goodnight,' came his low reply.

She climbed into bed. From where she lay she could see into part of Tammy's room, the foot of the little girl's bed and the length of Byron's bare legs where he'd thrust them out in front of him. She was fascinated by them, watched as he shifted in the chair to cross one bare ankle over the other.

What with Kym's change of heart and having Byron so close to her, she thought sleep would elude her but, surprisingly, knowing Byron was there calmed her, and her eyelids dropped. Vaguely, through the shrouds of sleep, she was aware of him standing up, stretching his cramped muscles, moving towards the door. She thought he paused by her doorway for long seconds before he passed on to his own room, but by then she was almost over the edge into a sound sleep, and couldn't be sure she hadn't dreamt it.

Rebecca had a picnic lunch ready by the time Byron came in from the west paddock next morning. Tammy seemed to be suffering no ill effects from her broken night; in fact, she hadn't mentioned her bad dream, but Rebecca spent an hour or so with her mid-morning reading her stories while she had a rest on her bed.

'Isn't it lovely that Daddy's coming too?' she beamed as she sat at the kitchen table, patiently waiting for her father to change out of his work clothes. 'I've never been to Stokes Bay before, but Mary, you know, Mary who looked after me when I came to Bay Ridge last holidays, well, Mary told me you have to walk under the rocks. Do you, Becca?' she asked, round-eyed.

'Yes, but it's not far and quite exciting,' Rebecca made light of it. 'I used to feel like an explorer finding an unknown path when I walked through it. And sometimes I pretended I was a pirate in search of buried treasure.'

Tammy giggled. 'You're funny, Becca.'

'And did you ever find any?' Byron's deep voice made her spin around as he entered the room.

He had shed his jeans and flannel shirt for faded denim shorts and a loose towelling T-shirt, and he wore sneakers like Rebecca and Tammy.

'Any what?' she asked, trying to drag her eyes away from the purely physical magnetism he exuded.

'Treasure,' he chuckled. 'Gold dubloons and pieces of eight.'

She shook her head. 'No. But we had a great time looking.'

'We?' His eyebrows rose.

'Rudy and I, usually. And our friends. We had beach parties there when we were teenagers. That was fun, too.' She smiled reminiscently. They had been good times, before her father was killed, when things were either black or white, and life was filled with simple, unadulterated pleasures.

'Do your friends still live here on the island, Becca?' Tammy asked.

'Some of them, I guess.' Rebecca smiled at her. 'But I've lost touch with them since I went over to the mainland.' For no reason at all she thought of Davie Kelly, and her eyes went back to Byron.

'Well, let's go.' He turned and picked up the picnic basket.

'Becca says we're going in her car, Daddy.' Tammy danced excitedly after her father.

'Oh, does she?' Byron turned to glance at Rebecca as she closed the back door.

'I thought it would be easier, as I know the way. I won't have to direct you.' Their eyes held. 'If that's all right with you?'

His lips moved in a faint smile. 'Lead on, Miss Grainger,' he said easily, and Tammy giggled delightedly.

'That sounds funny, calling Becca Miss Grainger,' she laughed as she climbed into the back of the pale orange Laser. 'It makes Becca sound like a school teacher.'

The road to Stokes Bay was unsealed, and this at least meant Rebecca had to concentrate on her driving, leaving Tammy and Byron to carry most of the conversation. With the little girl's constant chatter from the back seat, there was no need for Rebecca or Byron to add much, only an explanation here and there as Tammy plied her father with a chain of queries.

'What's that, Daddy?' she pointed to a brown ball moving slowly across the road in front of them.

'An echidna,' Byron told her as Rebecca slowed the car and pulled on to the verge. They got out for a closer look.

'It's all spikey, like a porcupine,' declared Tammy as the little creature reached the mound of the bank off the road and began to burrow into the gravelly dirt. 'Look at all those prickles, Becca.'

'It's also called the spiny anteater,' Byron explained. 'See its snout—and it has a long, sticky tongue for trapping the ants.'

Tammy was fascinated, and questioned Byron further as they continued on their way.

When they pulled into the bay, Tammy stared open-mouthed. 'But there's no sand, only rocks. Can't we build sandcastles, Becca?' she asked disappointedly.

'We're not quite there, love,' Rebecca reassured her. 'We have to walk the rest of the way. See those rocks? The bay is behind them, so we have to follow the path through them.'

'Oh.' Tammy climbed out of the car and eyed the rocky outcrop uncertainly. 'Are you sure we can get through them, Becca?'

'Mmm. Now, do you think you can manage your towel as well as your bucket and spade?'

Byron put the beach umbrella on his shoulder and picked up the picnic hamper, which only left the small bag containing Tammy's and Becca's change of clothes for Rebecca to carry. There was only one other car parked nearby, a campervan, and a middle-aged couple were making a cup of tea inside. They smiled as Rebecca, Byron and Tammy walked past them.

'We're going to have a picnic,' Tammy told them. 'And we're going right through those rocks.'

'Well, I never!' exclaimed the woman, smiling at Tammy. 'I'm going to stand here and watch you disappear with your mummy and daddy.'

Tammy laughed and threw a teasing glance at Rebecca before replying, 'OK. 'Bye.'

At the entrance to the rock path, Tammy turned and waved to the other woman, before taking Rebecca's hand and following her into the walkway between the huge limestone boulders. The trail wound snakewise under and through the rocky outcrops, and finally came out into the bright sunlight again.

The sandy beach stretched before them, disappearing like a pure white ribbon around the bay, skirted by high, jagged cliffs on the right and the deep blue of Investigator Strait on the left. A line of rocks ran parallel with the cliffs just off the beach, forming a natural and safe swimming lagoon of clear, rippling, pale turquoise water.

'Very nice,' murmured Byron appreciatively as they walked along the sand, deciding where to set up the beach umbrella.

They had the beach to themselves, and as the sea breeze stirred Rebecca's hair she reflected it wasn't hard to imagine they were the only people on earth, cradled in the outstretched arms of the rough cliffs, held captive on the white sand by the rolling waves.

'Can we swim now, Becca?' Tammy asked excitedly, and she nodded, helping the little girl slip out of her shorts and top which she'd worn over her swimming togs. Rebecca applied a liberal amount of sunscreen to Tammy's exposed skin and sat her hat firmly on her head. When she reached for the zinc cream, Tammy screwed up her nose.

'Ugh! Do I have to, Becca?'

'You don't want that beautiful little nose to peel, do you?' Rebecca asked as she smeared the cream on the little girl's face.

'What about yours?' Tammy asked, crossing her eyes as she tried to look at her lime-green nose.

'Becca doesn't want her beautiful little nose to peel either,' said Byron, and he took the tube from Rebecca's hand and began applying it to her nose, his lips controlling a smile. 'There!' He handed her the tube.

'And Daddy's, Becca,' directed Tammy. 'Do Daddy's, too.'

'Oh, well, he can do his own,' she said, offering him the tube, but Byron leaned forward and pointed to his nose.

'It wouldn't do to be odd man out,' he laughed, and Rebecca had to move forward and squeeze some of the cream on to her finger.

Kneeling before him, she reached out and ran the cream down the length of his nose, keeping her attention rigidly on her finger as she smoothed the cream over his skin. He was so tanned that she suspected his nose, like the rest of him, was quite safe from sunburn, and she could feel the silent amusement in his body.

Not so her own body. Her nerve-endings clamoured as a slow fire began to race through her, gathering excited momentum. Being this close to him did disastrous things to her control.

Her eyes were drawn to his, and she could see each minute detail of their deep blueness, of the fine, dark hair of his thick, curling lashes, of the thin laughter-lines radiating from the corners of his eyes, of that small scar on his cheekbone. Her breathing quickened, and the urge to touch the ridge of that scar almost overwhelmed her.

Somewhere in the distance of her awareness she heard Tammy scamper away, dancing on the water's edge as she splashed in the water, but Rebecca couldn't seem to move. Then, to her horror, her hand moved of its own accord and her fingertip traced the scar, moving softly over his skin.

CHAPTER TEN

SHE had to say something, or she'd make a complete fool of herself. Hurriedly, she swallowed.

'Did you get that playing football?' she asked, her voice high and thin.

For immeasurable seconds Byron remained silent, his eyes now darkly brooding, and then his lips twisted self-derisively and he turned away from her. 'No. Not that particular scar.'

Rebecca's whole body seemed to freeze as she felt him shut her away from him. His tone in itself was a douche of cold water to her heated body. He was spreading out his towel and, after removing his shirt, he lay back in the sun and closed his eyes.

Slowly Rebecca twisted the top back on the tube of zinc cream and, her heart heavy, she left him to join Tammy on the water's edge as she happily dug a moat around her sandcastle.

Byron set out their picnic lunch and called Rebecca and Tammy back to the shade of the umbrella to eat. As he laughed with his daughter, there was nothing left of the dark mood of half an hour ago. After they'd eaten their sandwiches, Tammy took her apple and went in search of shells, while Rebecca collected the leftovers to replace them in the basket.

'Becca, I'm sorry,' Byron's voice drew her downcast eyes to his face. 'For before.'

'That's OK. I didn't mean to pry.' She swallowed painfully.

'No, I know you didn't. It was a simple question, and you didn't deserve to be snapped at the way I did.' His

146

finger absently rubbed the scar and he sighed. 'I don't talk about it——'

'Oh, please. You don't have to now,' Rebecca broke in. 'I mean, if you don't want to...'

He was silent for a moment as he picked up a handful of sand and let it slide through his fingers. 'It was flying glass,' he said, 'or more accurately, *a* flying glass. Nikki, my wife, threw it at me.'

'Oh!' Rebecca breathed, totally astounded. 'I'm sorry.'

'I guess I'd slowed up. Usually I managed to duck the missiles she aimed at my head.' His lips twisted. 'Our marriage, Nikki's and mine, wasn't exactly the kind they call made in heaven. More like pure hell. For both of us.'

'Byron, you don't have to——' Rebecca began, her voice tight in her chest.

'I'd like to, if you'd care to listen,' he said, and Rebecca nodded as she sank down on the sand. 'Unfortunately, Tammy's the casualty of our battles. We married because——' he stopped, his eyes staring out over the water '—I married her because she was the most beautiful woman I'd ever seen. I fell for her like a ton of bricks.'

A tiny pain cut deep inside Rebecca.

'God knows why she married me,' he continued. 'Probably because she liked the razzmatazz that went with top-grade football, and while the parties went on we lived on the crest of the wave.' He turned back to Rebecca. 'But when we came down to earth it was totally impossible. So you see, Tammy was caught there between us and——' he rubbed his jaw '—her nightmares are a result of it all.'

'But Laurel says she hardly ever suffers from them now,' Rebecca put in.

Byron shook his head. 'The damage is still there, Becca. Otherwise she wouldn't have reacted the way she did when she heard us arguing last night. It brought it all back to her, and caused the recurrence of her nightmares.'

Rebecca didn't know what to say.

Byron watched Tammy approaching. 'Nikki and I have a lot to answer for,' he said softly, and then Tammy was reaching out her hand, showing him the pebbles she'd picked up on the sand.

'Did you really play pirates here when you were a little girl, Becca?' Tammy asked as she sat by the water between Rebecca and her father.

'Yes. And now I look at those cliffs, I shudder to think what would have happened if we'd fallen while we climbed all over them.'

'You climbed up there?' Tammy's eyes were round.

'Well, part of the way. We'd hide and pretend we could see the ships coming in to bury their treasure.' Rebecca laughed. 'Although bringing a ship in here would have been hazardous, to say the least. This whole section of the Australian coastline is really treacherous.'

'I believe there are quite a few shipwrecks around Kangaroo Island,' Byron remarked.

'Dozens. The *Mimosa* went down just out there in 1884. But probably the most notable wreck was the *Loch Vennacher* which sailed into the cliffs just north of West Bay in 1905. I remember when her remains were discovered in 1976. The waters around the island are pretty notorious, so the lighthouses play a big part in protecting ships from the rocks and reefs. It must have been terrifying sailing in the days before the lighthouses were built.' Rebecca shuddered.

'Do you think pirates really buried their treasure here?' Tammy asked and Rebecca laughed.

'Well, if they did it's still safe, because no one's ever found it. At least, Rudy and I never did.'

After their swim they lay on their towels to dry off, and Tammy was soon sound asleep. Rebecca closed her eyes and dozed for a little while herself. Eventually she sat up to check that Tammy was still in the lengthening shade of the umbrella.

Byron lay stretched out on his towel, one tanned arm flung over his eyes, and she allowed herself to look at him, let her eyes linger over the long, hard length of him. She swallowed painfully, wishing she could stretch out beside him, run her hands over his suntanned, salty skin, feel her fingertips curl, feather-soft, in the fine, dark hair on his chest.

He'd said before that he didn't know why Nikki had married him. Looking at him, at the smooth contours of his taut body, Rebecca understood exactly why the other girl had been attracted to him. What woman wouldn't be drawn to him? He was the most magnetic man Rebecca had ever met.

And she loved him. Maybe every bit as much as he'd loved his beautiful wife. A pain stabbed, clutching at her heart, filling her with a heavy, dejecting regret.

Byron moved then, his arm going to his side, and his eyes met hers, held her gaze, and neither of them could look away. She saw the flame flare in their dark blue depths and knew he found an answering glow in her own.

Rebecca caught her bottom lip between her teeth and she let her gaze fall to the throb of a pulse beating at the corner of his mouth. She looked up again and they continued to gaze into each other's eyes for timeless moments. There was a tightness in Rebecca's chest and her nerve-endings tingled, her body screaming out to feel the length of his against her. They were enveloped in their own circle of tension, and the air between them seemed to crackle with an electrified awareness.

Tammy stirred and murmured, and the sound of her voice cut between them like a knife severing the thickening air.

Rebecca swallowed painfully, wondering if her heartbeats could have actually ceased in those infinite moments, for now they thundered in her chest at breakneck pace.

Byron sat up and his hand moved towards her, his mouth a tense line, and in blind panic Rebecca pushed herself to her feet and began to shake out her sandy towel, not looking at Byron, for she was afraid she'd let herself take this moment out of time, without thought of tomorrow. Or yesterday. And the most beautiful woman Byron had ever seen.

Tammy woke up then, and they packed everything up to head home. Byron's face was remote as he led the way in to the rock tunnel.

At dinner the little girl happily told Jock and Kym all about their afternoon, about seeing the echidna, about the twisting pathway through the rocks; and, if Byron and Rebecca rarely added anything to the conversation, neither Jock nor Kym commented.

Instead of retiring to his room to watch television after dinner, Kym followed Rebecca through to the living-room while Byron read his daughter a bedtime story.

'You don't mind if I sit and talk a while, do you, Becca?' he asked, folding his long body into a chair.

'Of course not,' she replied as she picked up a shirt of Tammy's she was mending. Actually, she was quite relieved that she wouldn't have to make a pretence of sitting here with Byron before she could retire to bed.

'To tell you the truth, I was getting a bit sick of my own company. And I feel kind of bad about being such a dumbo.' He grinned sheepishly and shoved a cushion into the small of his back. 'Jock let me drive the bull-dozer today, and I think my spine has developed some form of metal fatigue.' He laughed. 'I'm discovering muscles I never knew I had tucked away.'

They were in the middle of a discussion on the merits of various current physical fitness fads when Byron joined them. He sat down in his chair and buried himself in his newspaper. Kym raised his eyebrows and indicated

Byron's obvious ill-humour. Rebecca shrugged, biting off a chuckle as Kym pulled a face that made him look very like his brother. The newspaper rustled disapprovingly and Kym grimaced, giving a theatrical yawn.

'Well, I'd best get to bed. Another big day tomorrow, if my back holds out,' he groaned. ''Night, Big Brother. Goodnight, Becca.' He leant forward and kissed her noisily on the cheek before winking at her as he left the room.

Rebecca set down her mending and stood up. 'I think I'll get to bed, too. All that sun and fresh air has made me sleepy.' And besides, she didn't want to sit here alone with Byron, not after those moments on the beach.

'Becca, before you go——' His voice halted her as she took a couple of steps towards the door.

She knew she should ignore him, but she could hardly do that. It would look decidedly odd if she cut and ran from him the way her every impulse directed her to do. So she stopped where she was, almost in the doorway, and slowly turned her head to look back at him.

'Yes?' she said, her voice tightening.

He didn't speak for what seemed like painfully long seconds, and Rebecca's hand, resting on the doorframe, tensed until the knuckles showed white. He folded the newspaper and threw it on the coffee-table, before pushing himself lithely to his feet to stand facing her.

'Did you enjoy yourself this afternoon?' he asked, and she blinked in surprise. Whatever she'd expected, it hadn't been that.

'Yes, of course,' she got out.

He nodded. 'I did, too.' His eyelids half masked the expression in his eyes, but Rebecca could feel his gaze fall over the length of her body clad in her soft, pastel pink, terry-towelling tracksuit, and her muscles tensed even more. She was so achingly aware of him that it was almost a physical pain. 'So did Tammy.'

Rebecca managed a smile. 'Yes, she did, didn't she? She couldn't stop chattering about it at dinner.'

'She likes you. You're good for her, Becca,' he said, and she thought she caught a slight unevenness in his tone.

Perhaps he wasn't quite as self-possessed, as in command of himself as she had imagined him to be. Her heart lurched.

'She's never had anyone give her as much undivided attention before. Oh, Laurel was wonderful with her, but she had her own two as well. And Nikki couldn't have cared if she lived or died,' he finished bitterly. 'I want you to know I appreciate it, Becca.'

'That's all right.' Rebecca swallowed unevenly. 'It's not hard to be with her; she's a wonderful little girl.' Wonderful. Just like her father, the thought sprang into life in her mind, and her heartbeats faltered heavily.

Was he as hyped up as she was? Was he conscious of her all but heedless need to reach out for him, to feel his lips on hers, his strong arms crushing her to him?

Of its own accord her gaze was lured back to his face, and with a shock she saw the naked wanting he wasn't quick enough to disguise. That same erratic pulse beat at the corner of his mouth, and his face looked pale and drawn.

He moved then, and she was incapable of fending him off. She stood immobile as he reached her in a couple of urgent strides, and when his arms closed around her she melted against him, unable to put up even a token resistance.

With a deep, husky groan he crushed her to his body, his lips finding hers in a fever of desperation. And they clung to each other, lost in each other, oblivious of everything around them. Byron's lips possessed hers, sparking a raging fire, and she responded with all the pent-up desire that had been dammed within her, had welled up inside her since those electric moments on the beach.

His hands caressed her back, slid sensuously beneath the waistband of her tracksuit top, his fingers tantalising her already heated skin. When his hand moved over her ribcage to mould one full breast, Rebecca moaned cravingly, her body curving against him. His thumb easily found her already erect nipple through the thin lace of her bra, sending wild tremors of yearning spiralling deliriously through her.

'I wanted to do this on the beach. God! How much I wanted it,' he said thickly as her body responded to his practised touch.

She was drowning in a sea of ecstatic sensations she had never suspected she could experience. Deftly he unclipped the front clasp of her bra and his fingers enveloped her bare flesh. Rebecca's senses soared still higher, impossibly higher than she'd ever imagined they could climb, and her own unsteady fingers fumbled with the buttons on his shirt before sliding inside to luxuriate in the elating touch of his hard body.

Her lips traced the strong, tanned sinews at the base of his throat, nuzzling light, teasing kisses over his chest as her hands insinuated themselves inside his shirt to wrap around him, her fingertips finding the valley of his backbone, deliberately caressing its length.

Byron was trembling, and she felt his arousal in every inch of his body. He held her slightly away from him, his breath catching in a ragged gasp as he gazed down at her naked breasts. His finger circled each rosy peak and then slowly he lowered his dark head, his tonguetip emulating the sensuous movement of his fingers.

Rebecca shuddered with delight, and when he lifted his head to meet her half-closed eyes she had to fight back the almost overwhelming desire to beg him not to stop, to go on for ever, to carry them both away on this crazily breathtaking, indescribably beautiful rapport.

'Becca. Becca,' he breathed against the curve of her throat. 'You're driving me insane, do you know that? Totally insane.'

She murmured low in her throat as the deep huskiness of his voice incited her further. Her breasts were pressed provocatively against the hair-roughened skin of his bare chest, and his hands drew her hips into the aroused curve of his taut thighs.

'I want you, Becca,' his voice rasped thickly, 'more than I thought I could want a woman again.' He kissed her hard on the lips, then gently on her brow, her eyelids, the tip of her nose. 'I want to kiss every inch of you, make love to you until we're both too exhausted to move.'

Rebecca's heart soared inside her and she stirred sensually against him.

She knew she was perilously close to not being able to keep her head, and she drew a little away from him. 'Byron, we shouldn't ... We have to stop—I can't ...'

Byron caught his breath, and with a raw, broken groan his hands cupped her face. 'And I can't take much more of this either, Becca. I can see only one solution.' The pad of one thumb followed the sensitive outline of her lips. 'I'm tired of casual affairs; I don't want that with you. And I somehow can't see Jock approving of it.' The corner of his mouth lifted crookedly. 'So I think we'd better carry Jock's matchmaking plans out to the letter, and get married,' he said, the corners of his mouth twisting derisively. 'And pretty damn quickly.'

CHAPTER ELEVEN

A COLDNESS began to clutch at Rebecca's very soul. He said he was tired of affairs, and he would have had his share of those, she thought self-derisively. And had they met in any other situation she would have joined the ranks of those other nameless women.

Byron wanted her, and he was prepared to marry her to get her. He couldn't see he'd have her any other way, not with an old-fashioned grandfather like Jock watching his every move. Especially one who had subtly manoevred them together in the first place.

In those few seconds, a profusion of disjointed thoughts pulled torturously at her heart. Her grandfather's matchmaking, Tammy's need for a stable situation, Byron's feelings for his beautiful wife... But never love.

The pain grew worse. But what about love? she wanted to scream at him. Wanting and loving were two vastly different emotions. Teamed together, they made for rapturous happiness, a happiness she had almost clasped in her hands, only to see it now slipping so easily through her fingers. If there was no love, what remained when the first desperate wanting faded?

Rebecca's whole body stilled, and she took a step away from him. Byron let her go, his eyes carefully watching her pale face. She shivered, and realised her breasts were still bare from their feverish lovemaking. Flushing, she turned away from him, reclasping her bra and straightening her tracksuit top.

'Becca?' There was a question in his voice, and she swallowed the lump of tears that threatened to choke her.

'I . . . think we should call it a night. It's late and you have to be up early, don't you?'

'Rebecca.' This time his tone brooked no argument, and his fingers closed firmly on her arm, swinging her back to face him. 'Rebecca, I asked you to marry me. I'd say that deserves some kind of answer, wouldn't you?'

Reluctantly she looked up at him, and that was a mistake, for she almost weakened, very nearly threw herself into his arms and cried, yes, she'd marry him, on any terms he'd like to dictate. But she steeled herself with a mighty effort and dropped her gaze to the square jut of his chin.

She shook her head. 'No, Byron.'

His fingers on her arm tightened painfully, and she flinched, wrenching away from him.

'What kind of an answer is that?' he demanded, and he was quite pale around his mouth.

'I can't marry you. I'm sorry, but——' She bit her lip. 'It wouldn't work.'

'You can't mean that. A moment ago it was working, as you put it, pretty bloody well.'

'No.' She moved her head in denial.

'No? You're sorry? It wouldn't work?' His laugh was short and derisive and he swore sharply. 'I could have taken you just then, Rebecca. And if I touched you now——'

'No.' She took another step away from him, coming up against the doorjamb. 'My God! You're an arrogant, self-centred——' She drew a shredded breath. 'The marvellous Byron Willoughby thinks he only has to snap his fingers and women fall all over him. Well, not this one. Oh, I admit you have the experienced technique to turn me on, but so do plenty of other men. When I marry, I want more than just a superstud for a husband. I——'

'That's enough, Rebecca,' he bit out through clenched teeth. 'I don't think you need to take it any further. Let's just say I get the message. Loud and clear. Now get out of my sight before I do something I suspect I wouldn't even regret.'

Rebecca went. And she was still sleepless when the household began to stir next morning.

Two days later, she felt no lifting of the depression that had settled upon her. She could hear movement in the kitchen, Jock laughing with Tammy, and she paused in the hallway, gently massaging her temples. Her head throbbed and her body ached with the constant strain of their animosity, hers and Byron's, of just being with him. When they were alone his eyes looked straight through her, and she knew she would be unable to take much more of the impossible situation.

The rain that had continued most of last night was still falling when they awoke, so Jock and Byron had taken the opportunity to spend the morning in the shed overhauling one of the tractors, while Kym was despatched into town to collect some of the parts that were needed.

Out the back a car door slammed, and then she heard Kym's voice eagerly addressing his brother. Since the night Tammy had had her nightmare, Kym's attitude to Byron had begun to alter, and as Rebecca made herself move towards the kitchen she reflected wryly that at least the brothers were on much friendlier terms.

'Hi, Becca!' Kym grinned at her and threw his arms around her, swinging her around in an exaggerated waltz.

'Kym, must you fool around?' Byron frowned irritably.

'Got to get in some practice for the dance.' He winked at Rebecca. 'With my favourite girl.'

'Such charm,' Rebecca managed lightly, all the while aware of Byron's obvious displeasure.

'Then this must be the best time to ask for one of your fantastic cups of tea. I'm parched.' Kym made a choking noise for emphasis.

'Now you're talking,' put in Jock, and Rebecca crossed to switch on the electric kettle.

Kym sat down facing his brother. 'Byron, I've had this fantastic chance to go fishing—well, cray fishing actually,' he began enthusiastically.

'Now steady on, lad,' Jock admonished him. 'I thought you went into town for the tractor parts.'

'I did. They're in the car, Jock. But I had this amazing stroke of luck. You'll never believe it.'

Byron took a mouthful of tea. 'You'd better begin at the beginning.'

'Well, I was in getting the parts, and when I said put it on Bay Ridge's account, this guy next to me asked me if I worked here. I told him I was your brother et cetera, and that I was helping out. Then we got on to fishing, and he said he'd give me a job on his boat for his next trip, because one of his deckhands wants a bit of time off to get married.'

Rebecca poured herself a cup of tea, but remained standing by the counter, watching Kym's animated face. There was no resemblance to the sulky boy she'd met at Laurel's.

'When's this trip likely to be?' Byron was asking.

'Leaving Monday. Do you mind if I go? I can earn some cash as well as get some experience, and you don't really need me in the west paddock any longer, do you?'

'It's just about done now,' Jock corroborated, and Byron frowned, tapping his fingertips on the table-top.

'How long will the trip last?'

'About a week or so. It's a fantastic opportunity, Byron,' Kym emphasised.

'Who owns the boat?'

'The guy who offered me the job. It's his own boat.'
He turned to smile at Rebecca. 'He said he's an old friend
of Rebecca's, actually. A tall, nice-looking bloke called
Davie Kelly. An old flame, Becca?'

Rebecca caught Jock's eye and her grandfather had
the grace to look at little discomfited, but when her gaze
shifted to Byron his eyes raked her glacially, twisting her
stomach muscles into knots. She set her tea down,
knowing if she attempted to swallow it she'd choke.

'Do you remember him, Becca?' Kym was asking her
mischievously.

'He was a friend of my brother's more than a friend
of mine,' she replied stiltedly, not looking at Byron.

'He's got a good solid boat,' Jock put in, 'and does
pretty well for himself with it.'

'So what do you think, Byron?' Kym appealed to his
brother. 'I'd like to take the job if you can spare me
from the farm.'

Byron shrugged. 'If that's what you want to do, and
as long as you realise what you're in for. It won't be a
pleasure cruise.'

'I know.' Kym beamed. 'Davie explained what I'd have
to do. He's calling round just after lunch to see if I'll
take the job. I offered to phone him, but,' he grinned,
'I think he wanted the excuse to come out to Bay Ridge,
for some inexplicable reason.' He cast a teasing glance
at Rebecca. 'I can't imagine what that would be.'

The rasping noise of Byron's chair scraping back as
he stood up cut across Kym's amusement, and Byron
strode towards the door.

'Come on, I want to get the tractor finished,' he said
sharply, not waiting to see if they followed him.

Jock went out after him, but Kym paused by the door
to turn and wink at Rebecca. 'I reckon Big Brother's
absolutely green with jealousy,' he confided in a stage
whisper before he continued out after the other two.

Rebecca sat down to finish her tea, absently watching Tammy, who was happily engaged with a colouring book and crayons.

Byron, jealous? Rebecca's lips twisted cynically. Kym was wrong. Byron had simply been thwarted and he didn't like it. He'd had it all worked out. A permanent babysitter for his daughter and a woman in his bed.

She shivered responsively at the thought. No, he wasn't jealous. He'd have to care to be suffering from that emotion. She caught her thoughts together and forced them determinedly away from Byron Willoughby.

Davie Kelly. Two years ago he had been the catalyst, the ingredient added to the volatile situation on Bay Ridge between Jock and herself.

That final argument with her grandfather had blown up, gathering momentum after weeks of disagreements. And their battles had grown louder and more bitter.

Then Jock had suggested, after one difference of opinion between them, that at almost twenty years old it was time Rebecca thought about getting married, implying that marriage might sweeten her up.

In the beginning she had laughed it off, but as time went on she had grown tired of the joke, angrily telling Jock she had no time for marriage, that she simply wasn't interested. And anyway, she'd thrown at him, just who on the island was exciting enough for her to marry? None of the young men she knew did a thing for her, and if three or four had tried to gain her attention she had politely but firmly said, thanks, but no thanks. So word had got around.

Davie Kelly, Jock had stated out of the blue. His grandfather was a friend of Jock's, and he was a presentable enough lad.

Rebecca had laughed. Davie Kelly was a friend of Rudy's, but apart from that dubious honour she didn't like him. Oh, physically he was quite attractive. He had a fine head of rusty-coloured hair and twinkling blue eyes. They'd even gone out together a couple of times, but since the night he'd had a little too much to drink and got amorous with her in a maudlin way, Rebecca had given him the cool treatment.

Her grandfather had persisted. Davie Kelly had his own cray-boat just like his father, and he was doing extremely well with it. If she married Davie Kelly she'd be set up for life. The Kellys were a good church-going family, and many a girl would jump at the chance.

Not this girl, Rebecca had replied forcefully. Besides, what made Jock think Davie Kelly was even interested in her? she'd laughed.

Oh, he's interested, Jock had retorted. Jock had spoken to Davie's father, and the family were more than happy with the idea. They thought it was time Davie married, too.

Rebecca had been horrified. To think that they had all arranged her marriage, as though she was a cosseted Victorian maiden!

For once Rudy had seemed to side with Jock. What was wrong with Davie Kelly? He was Rudy's mate. A good bloke.

That had been the last straw for Rebecca. Why don't you dress me in a flour sack and set me up to go to the highest bidder? she'd cried at them, and then retreated to her room, angry and tearful.

Instead of being deterred, Jock had continued to pressure her with his usual tenacity. He had invited Davie and his parents to dinner. Rebecca hadn't exactly been rude to them, but the atmosphere over that dinner-table had not been relaxed. The black looks Jock surreptitiously sent Rebecca did not bode well for her when their guests left. Rebecca only wanted to escape.

And after dinner it had been Davie who suggested she show him the new colt. Walking with Davie instead of sitting making polite conversation she'd considered to be the lesser of the two evils. She'd get the chance to discuss the problem with Davie, nip it all in the bud. After all, Davie liked girls, plural, and Rebecca was sure he would be as averse to a marriage as she was.

They'd dutifully admired the colt and, as Rebecca sought a way to bring the conversation around to their marriage, she'd looked up to find Davie's eyes on her rather speculatively.

'I guess you know about our prospective marriage?' he'd said without preamble. 'What do you think of the idea?'

'The same as you do,' Rebecca burst out. 'I'm so angry with Jock, I could spit chips. He has no right to embarrass us like this.'

'I'm not embarrassed.'

'Well, I am.'

'There's no need to be, Becca. It's not such a bad idea, really. We could do worse.'

Rebecca stared up at him in surprise. 'You can't mean...?'

'That I'm *for* the idea? Why not? I wouldn't mind a wife at home, warm slippers, warm bed...'

Rebecca flushed. 'We hardly know each other.'

'We've known each other since we were kids. What's to know? I think we'd do each other fine.' Davie leant forward and brushed her lips with his own.

Shock held Rebecca motionless, and Davie took her quiescence for acquiescence. His arms slid around her and he pulled her against him, his mouth seeming to devour hers. Rebecca was galvanised into action, and she began to struggle against him. For a moment she thought he wasn't going to release her, but he let her go and she stepped backwards.

'Don't ever do that again,' she bit out angrily.

'Hell, what's with you, Becca? What's wrong with a little kiss?'

'I just don't care to be grabbed and pawed.'

Davie's face flushed. 'There is something wrong with you, Becca. None of the other girls I know "don't care to be grabbed and pawed",' he mimicked sarcastically.

'I'm not some other girl, I'm me.'

Davie's eyes narrowed. 'OK. Be like that. But don't expect me to dally around begging for your pretty little favours. You can find some other namby-pamby. And come to think of it, Becca, I've changed my mind. I don't need a wife anyway, so they'll have to palm you off on someone else.'

And as if that hadn't been enough, a week or so later at the local dance Rebecca overheard Davie discussing her with a couple of his mates, telling them his parents wanted him to settle down. With Becca Grainger, of all sheilas.

'Thought you'd been out with her a couple of times?' remarked one of the others.

'I have. And believe me, she's a cold fish,' Davie said. 'I reckon she's frigid, not worth a bloke's time or trouble.'

'Hell! Who'd have guessed it? She's not a bad-looking bird, either. Just shows how a guy can get sucked in. I was going to ask her out myself.'

'Take it from me, save yourself the trouble. And they can forget about marriage. If Becca thinks I'm going to get roped into it she's got another think coming,' Davie vowed. 'Marriage! Hell, I'm too young to die.'

The next time Jock brought up the subject she'd exploded at him, telling him he wasn't her keeper, that she was of age and would look after her own life. If he persisted with his ridiculous scheme to pair her off with Davie Kelly, or anyone else for that matter, she'd leave the farm.

Jock had been as angry as she had been by then, and taunted her that she wouldn't be able to manage on her own, that she'd come running back so fast they wouldn't even know she'd gone.

Was that so? Rebecca had been icily calm then. Well, she'd prove Jock wrong. She was leaving and, what was more, she was never coming back. Not ever. Not if they begged her to return.

So she'd gone. The very next day. And the first few months had been totally miserable. In her tiny flat in Adelaide she'd cried with homesickness, for the farm and Rudy and Jock. But her vehement statement that she could manage on her own, that she wasn't coming back, had made her stick it out. Her pride had won out.

She'd forced herself to join in the city life-style. She'd gone to an endless string of parties, innumerable discos, met lots of young men whom she kept quite happily at arm's length, for she wasn't giving anyone else the chance to brand her as frigid or otherwise. She was free. Of the farm, of the island, of the boring Davie Kelly, and of Jock.

When she had been asked to make the move to Sydney with the transfer of the company's head office, she'd done so with scarcely a qualm, for there wasn't really anyone who made the parting difficult. By then she'd conditioned herself into not missing the open spaces, the windswept beauty of Bay Ridge, the island, and her family...

Davie Kelly arrived just after Byron, Jock and Kym returned from working on the tractor. He looked exactly as Rebecca remembered him, with a mop of rusty-coloured hair and laughing blue eyes, the light of the devil in them. Although he was six feet tall, he was still a couple of inches shorter than Byron.

He made a show of giving Rebecca a bear hug and kissing her soundly on the cheek. 'Great to see you again, Becca. I heard you were home. How long will you be staying?'

'I'm not sure,' she told him, very much aware of Byron's set face, his cold eyes watching them.

'Going back to Sydney?'

'No, I don't think so. But I suppose I'll have to think about looking for another job. At the moment I'm helping Byron out looking after his daughter.'

'That means you'll be around for a while,' he said with obvious satisfaction, and smiled at her. 'Maybe we can get together and talk about old times.'

Rebecca had to smile back. Davie, it appeared, had a very short memory. Or perhaps he thought she'd had long enough to overcome her sad case of frigidity. However, even if she hadn't overheard his cruel words two years ago, he just wasn't her type. Not then and not now. Especially not now.

'Davie, this is my brother, Byron,' Kym said, and Davie turned away from Rebecca.

'Hi!' Davie held out his hand, and a little slowly Byron reached out to shake it. 'I think we met at the footie club a while ago, didn't we?'

Byron nodded unsmilingly. 'Kym tells me you've offered him a job?'

'Yes. I need a deckhand on my next trip.' He turned to Kym. 'Going to take it on?'

'You bet!' Kym grinned. 'Still leaving Monday?'

'Weather permitting.' Davie frowned thoughtfully. 'If it gets any worse than this, and the forecast says it won't, then we'll leave it a few days. I hope you don't suffer from seasickness.'

Kym shrugged. 'I never have before.'

Jock had pulled some cold cans of beer from the fridge for the men, and they began discussing the cray fishing industry, and from there the conversation moved to the waters around the island.

Davie told them the southern and western coasts were more hazardous because of the high cliffs, the reefs, and the rough surf, and Kym enthusiastically started to add the little he'd read on shipwrecks in the area. There had been over forty since the first recorded disaster in 1847. Rebecca kept her participation in the discussion to a minimum, but she was conscious of Davie's teasingly admiring glances, and even more aware of the shuttered frostiness in Byron's eyes when he was forced to look at her.

'I guess you'll be coming to the dance tomorrow night.' Davie glanced at Rebecca and her eyes widened in surprise. 'At the footie club,' he said by way of explanation.

'Oh, no,' Rebecca was uneasily aware of Byron's swift glance and set expression. 'I don't think I'll be able to make it.'

'Why not?' queried Kym. 'Jock said we were all going. You're coming, aren't you, Byron? I thought we'd decided the other night at dinner.'

Byron's eyes slid over Rebecca again and on to Davie, who sat back, smiling good-naturedly. 'As you say, why not?' Byron shrugged. 'We'll be making a party of it. They arrange games for the kids, so Tammy will enjoy it.'

Rebecca opened her mouth to decline again, and then thought better of it. Why shouldn't she go? It might be fun to see some of her friends again.

By the time Davie took his leave, with a promise to see Rebecca at the dance the following evening, it was time to prepare their dinner. Kym stayed chatting to her about his proposed trip with Davie, while Byron disappeared outside with Jock.

'Big Brother is not a happy man,' Kym stated. 'I've never known him to be so cantankerous. Jock told him he needed a good night's sleep, but I won't tell you what Byron said to that.'

Rebecca looked up from dicing the vegetables, and Kym raised his eyebrows expressively.

'It would make a sailor blush,' he said.

'Maybe he is tired,' she said carefully.

'He's been decidedly grumpy these past few days. Wonder what's responsible for his sleepless nights. Or should I say, who?' Kym eyed her thoughtfully, but she escaped into the pantry before he could make any further comment.

Later that evening, Rebecca was tiptoeing out of Tammy's room after checking on the sleeping little girl when she heard a car pull up outside. Who could be calling at this hour? She glanced at her wristwatch. It was almost eight o'clock.

Pulling Tammy's door closed, she walked down the hallway and flicked on the outside light before opening the door.

A man was stepping from a light-coloured utility, pausing to look up at Rebecca before closing the car door and starting towards the house. It wasn't until he reached the circle of light that Rebecca recognised him.

'Davie!' she said softly, her eyes wide with surprise. He had only left a few hours ago.

'Hello, Becca.' He walked up the steps and crossed the veranda towards her.

'Did you forget something?' she got out. 'About the fishing trip?'

He shook his head. 'No, I came back to see you. You know, we go way back and I didn't even welcome you back properly. After all these years I should have given you more than a peck on the cheek. I mean, we did almost tie the knot.' With that, he drew her into his arms and his lips closed over hers.

Rebecca stood frozen for seconds before she could move. Her hands came up to his chest and pushed against him as she twisted her head to one side to escape his lips. His arms still held her loosely, and as she stepped away from him she smelt the repelling odour of alcohol on his breath.

'Aren't you going to invite me in?' he asked as he reluctantly released her.

'I... Well, no. I don't think so, Davie.' She barred the door with her body.

'Come on, Becca. Where's your hospitality? This door was always open to the Kellys.' He stepped forward, and Rebecca had to move backwards. He walked into the living-room and, after a glance towards the back of the house, she followed him into the room. As far as Rebecca knew, Byron was still out in the shed.

Davie's movements were quite co-ordinated, but his fair complexion was flushed and his eyes were slightly red-rimmed. He sat down in Byron's chair and motioned for her to sit opposite him.

'I hoped I'd get to see you alone so we could talk about old times. What made you come back, Becca?'

'I was born here, just like you. It's my home.' She shrugged. 'Why shouldn't I come back?'

'You left in a pretty big hurry.' His eyes roved downwards over her body, and Rebecca crossed her arms. Davie's lips twisted. 'There was a whispered rumour going round at the time about the reason for your hasty disappearance.'

Rebecca straightened in her chair. 'What on earth are you talking about?'

Davie grinned. 'Everyone thought you were in the family way.'

Rebecca's jaw dropped. 'You can't be serious!'

'It's true. And everyone thought I was the culprit.'

'Why, that's...' Rebecca stood up and paced the carpet angrily. 'That's ridiculous.'

'Is it, Becca?' Davie asked teasingly.

'Of course it is. And you know damn well it is, Davie. I hope you told everyone it was impossible, too.' Rebecca faced him.

'What was the use in denying it? No one really believed me, anyway.'

Rebecca felt her cheeks burn and she fought the urge to slap his smiling face. 'Did Jock know about this?' she demanded, and Davie shrugged.

'I don't think anyone would have said anything to him. Well, they wouldn't, would they? Were you pregnant, Becca?' Davie stood up in front of her, and her shocked surprise momentarily overrode her anger.

'Of course I wasn't! How can you ask that? We didn't...' Rebecca flushed again.

'I wasn't the only guy on the island. And I often wondered. You know, you weren't a bad-looking bird. You still aren't.' His eyes fell to the rise of her breasts. 'Maybe you and I should pick up where we left off.' He reached for her, and his lips came down on hers before she could move away from him.

Nausea rose inside her and she pushed frantically against him. However, a loud cough from behind them was more successful in putting an end to Davie's repulsive kisses than Rebecca's struggles were. As Davie's hold on her relaxed, she pulled herself away from him to see Byron lounging easily in the doorway.

Davie turned his head to look from one to the other, and whatever he saw caused his lips to twist ruefully.

'Oh, I see,' he said good-naturedly. 'You have other fish to fry. Seems I've missed my chance again. Lady Luck's sure got it in for me.'

Rebecca cringed inside and then tensed as Byron walked into the room, his body as tautly poised as a panther about to pounce.

'Byron.' Her eyes implored him silently. 'Davie was just leaving, weren't you, Davie?' Rebecca moved closer to Byron, slipping her arm intimately through his, her body brushing his.

Byron's expression betrayed not a flicker of emotion at her actions, although she felt the tension in him.

Davie smiled again. 'Better look to your laurels, Will, because all's fair, you know. I just might give you something of a run for your money where Becca's concerned. And I've got a bit of a start on you. Becca and I go way back, and we had some good times together, didn't we, love?'

'I'll see you out, Kelly.' Byron motioned towards the door.

After Byron had closed the door behind Davie, Rebecca let out a sigh of relief, and she glanced apologetically up at him. 'I'm sorry I had to——' She paused.

'Use me to get rid of your ex-boyfriend?' he finished caustically. 'Oh, don't mention it, Rebecca. Any time I can be of service,' he added coldly as he left her and disappeared into his room.

CHAPTER TWELVE

THE next day Byron's temper grew worse, until even Tammy was walking warily around him. The rain fell again, keeping the men from working out in the west paddock, so it was with some reluctance that Rebecca dressed for the dance that night.

She deliberated over what to wear, her fingers idly flicking through the clothes hanging in her wardrobe until she eventually settled on a pretty lemon dress, the colour a perfect foil for her dark hair and lightly tanned complexion.

Slipping the soft material over her head, she smoothed the dress over her hips and tied the belt. It was just right for her. With her high-heeled white sandals and a matching clutch bag, she was satisfied she looked her best. And, coming home later, she would need her white crocheted shawl to keep her warm when the night grew chilly.

She checked her light make-up and brushed her hair. With a last wry look in the mirror, she left her room and crossed to Tammy's to help the little girl put on her own party dress.

The hall was brightly lit and the dance was going to be well attended, judging by the number of cars already parked in the paddock nearby. Byron eased the Commodore into a parking space and they all climbed out, Tammy skipping excitedly beside Rebecca. The rain had stopped, but the ground was soft underfoot, so they had to tread warily on the soggy ground.

In the semi-darkness Rebecca slanted a glance at Byron and her breath caught in her throat. He really was the most attractive man she had ever seen, and in that moment of intense clarity she desperately wished she'd accepted his proposal, that she could legitimately slip her arm through his and feel the warmth of his body beside hers.

His dark suit moulded his broad shoulders and was cut immaculately over his narrow waist and hips, and the material of his trousers hugged his muscular thighs, accentuating the long length of his legs. Rebecca was almost mesmerised. Only when he turned his head to look in her direction did she hastily tear her eyes from him.

For some reason she wanted to cry. Tears rushed into her eyes and she swiftly blinked them away, a tight pain clutching the region of her heart. She had to pull herself together before she faced the others, before she met Byron's gaze again.

People began to greet them as soon as they entered the hall, and Tammy clutched shyly at Rebecca's hand.

'Becca Grainger! We heard you were home.' A short, plumpish girl a little older than Rebecca walked up to them, her face alight with a wide smile. 'Remember me?'

Rebecca smiled back. 'Angie, how could I forget you?' she teased, and the other girl grimaced.

'Once seen, never forgotten,' she laughed. 'Hi, Jock. Byron.'

Byron introduced Kym and Tammy and the men moved off, leaving Rebecca and Tammy with Angie.

'Did Byron say Angie Kelly?' Rebecca asked in surprise.

'Mmm. I remarried eighteen months ago. To Pat Kelly. But tell me about yourself. How long have you been home?'

'A few weeks. I got a little browned off with city life and decided to come back here.'

'Well, it's great to see you again,' Angie assured her sincerely.

Rebecca had always liked Angie. In fact, she didn't know of anyone who didn't like the other girl, who had been tragically widowed when her baby daughter was a few months old.

'You look great. And all grown up,' Angie teased.

'You're not that much older than I am, remember?' laughed Rebecca. 'And you look pretty good, too.'

'All grown up as well, and grown out,' she grimaced self-derisively. 'That's what having three kids will do to you.'

'Three?'

'Yes.' Angie laughed. 'Susie will be six next week, then Pat and I have two boys, twins, just seven months old. The babies are a little young for these dos so they're being spoilt rotten by Pat's parents, but Susie's here. Come and meet her and Pat.' She led them across the hall, talking all the time. 'Remember Pat? He's Davie's older brother.' Angie's eyes twinkled teasingly. 'You do remember Davie, don't you, Becca?'

'Yes, I remember Davie,' she replied drily. And she vaguely remembered his brother, Pat. He was the eldest of the five Kellys, while Davie was the youngest.

'Pat's a wonderful guy, Becca,' Angie was saying, her face sobering, a trace of past sadness in her eyes. 'When Rob died I wanted to die, too. I guess I just drifted on because of Susie, but Pat convinced me I needed more than that. He was right, and I know Rob would have agreed with him.'

'I'm glad for you, Angie.'

'Thanks, Becca. I'm really happy. It took Pat a lot of smooth talking to convince me to marry him, and I'm just so glad he did.'

They joined a group of people, and Angie drew her husband forward. 'Here's Pat, Becca. Pat, you remember Becca Grainger, don't you?'

'Sure. Hi, Becca! Good to see you again,' Pat greeted her quietly. While Davie and Pat were both tall and red-headed, no two brothers could be more dissimiliar in personality. Pat was as shy and unassuming as Davie was outgoing.

'And this is Susie.' Angie drew her daughter forward. 'Becca's a friend of mine and this is Tammy. How about taking her over to the playroom to meet the other children?'

Tammy looked uncertainly up at Rebecca and her hand tightened in Rebecca's.

'Would you like me to come with you to see what they're going to be doing?' she asked, and Tammy nodded.

'I'll come, too,' said Angie, taking Susie's hand.

Rebecca turned towards Byron, trying to catch his eye. He seemed deep in conversation with Jock, Kym and a couple of other men, but he must have felt her eyes on him for he looked up immediately and, excusing himself, came towards her.

'I'm going to take Tammy over to meet the other children,' she told him, and he nodded unsmilingly before turning back to greet Pat Kelly.

'One of Pat's sisters will be looking after the children tonight,' Angie said as she fell into step beside them. 'We all take turns and it works really well.'

They approached a group of youngsters, and Tammy's face broke into a shy smile. With Susie's help she was coaxed into the group, and was soon playing with the other children.

'And what about you? No special man from the big city?' Angie asked as the two girls sat down off to the side.

Rebecca shook her head. 'No, I'm afraid not.'

'There must be something wrong with the men on the mainland,' Angie exclaimed, and Rebecca laughed. 'How long will you be staying? I hear you've left your job in Sydney.'

'Yes, and I was planning on getting another position in Adelaide so I could be near Jock, but I've agreed to look after Tammy for Byron until he can get a permanent babysitter,' she finished evenly.

Angie nodded. 'I believe his wife was killed in a car accident a couple of years ago. It's hard on a little girl to be without her mother, and Byron would need someone to look after Tammy when he's out working all day.'

'Yes,' Rebecca murmured uneasily.

'He seems a really nice guy. Byron Willoughby, I mean. Don't you think so, Becca?' Angie was watching her.

'I guess he is.'

'And handsome. Every girl's dream come true.'

'He is rather nice-looking,' she agreed, hoping Angie wouldn't notice her flushed face.

'You could say that.' Angie's knowing smile said Rebecca wasn't kidding her. 'One for the understatements, aren't you, love? He could put his shoes under my bed any time he likes.'

Rebecca laughed. 'Is that John Cronin over there? He was in my year at school,' she said, changing the subject.

'Mm, that's him. Amazing how those gangling youths grow up into reasonably presentable young men, isn't it?'

'With wives and families, too,' Rebecca added.

'Oh, not all of them.' Angie's eyes twinkled. 'Davie's not married yet, and I have a feeling he'll be pleased to see you here tonight.'

'Angie——' Rebecca began as the band burst forth with an old favourite. As if on cue, Davie Kelly materialised in front of them.

'Hi, Becca. How about we get the night off to a good start?' He laughed at her, taking her hand and pulling her on to her feet and into his arms. Rebecca only had time to see the pleased beam on Angie's face as she was whirled away.

'I don't really want to dance with you, Davie, after last night.' She frowned at him.

'Yeah, well, I'm sorry, Becca, I had a few too many and opened my big trap too wide.' Davie looked suitably contrite.

'Was it the truth, about everyone thinking I left because I was pregnant?'

Davie's eyes fell. 'A couple of the guys suggested it, but I soon shut them up. I was just needling you. Don't know why. Must have been the demon drink.'

'Well, I wasn't impressed at all,' she began, and he swung her around.

'Was I hallucinating last night, or did you also say you and Will were together?' Davie asked.

'Don't you remember?' Rebecca played for time.

'Maybe I just don't want to remember. You know I always fancied you, Becca, and I have to say you're even more attractive now than you used to be.' He drew a little away from her and gazed quizzically down at her. 'Nothing to say, Becca?'

'Thank you, Davie, for the compliment.' She had to smile. 'And you've not lost any of your Irish charm.'

Davie chuckled. 'With a name like Kelly, I have a reputation to uphold. But you didn't answer my question.'

'What question?'

'About you and Will, and how things stand.'

Rebecca's gaze fell to the knot of his tie. 'I told you last night.'

'He did look as though he wanted to tear me apart. The jealous type, is he?'

'I...no, I don't think so.'

'I know so. Take it from me, Becca, he's jealous as hell. In fact, he hasn't taken his eyes off us since we took to the floor.'

Rebecca went to pull away from him, her face flushing, but Davie held her fast.

'I was having you on, Becca, pulling your leg. Come on, let's just enjoy ourselves, like the old days.' Rebecca remained stiffly in his arms. 'Hey, Becca, what happened to your sense of humour?'

'That wasn't exactly the joke of the year,' she retorted drily.

'No, I guess not. Forgive me?' He looked earnestly down at her, and she shook her head exasperatedly.

'You really haven't changed a bit, have you, Davie?'

'Nope.' He laughed. 'Still twenty-six, going on fifteen.'

Rebecca laughed and relaxed a little. He really was incorrigible.

'Like old times, isn't it?' He smiled as he pulled her closer, his blue eyes twinkling devilishly.

'We had no old times, Davie Kelly, and you know it,' she told him with mock seriousness.

'Sure we did. I definitely remember a night after one of the dances I managed to manoeuvre you into a dark corner. I had evil thoughts on my mind too, but you soon put me very firmly in my place.' He chuckled. 'I still remember those dark eyes flashing at me.'

Rebecca laughed with him. 'Should I apologise? For resisting your manly technique, I mean?'

'Oh, absolutely. Wounded my fragile pride, you did. Hit me right in my ego.'

'Not your ego!' Rebecca raised her eyebrows expressively. 'Then I apologise profusely.' She glanced up at him through her lashes. 'Can't say I can see any evidence of permanent damage.'

'Ah! That's the Becca I remember.' He pulled her close and kissed her on the cheek before swinging her round as the dance came to an end.

Rebecca laughingly tried to catch her breath as Davie led her off the floor, and they almost walked into Byron.

He was standing with arms folded, watching the dancing, and his face was totally devoid of expression.

'Hi, Will,' Davie greeted him jovially before turning back to Rebecca. 'Thanks for the dance, Becca. I'll leave you in safe hands. I see a mate of mine I want to catch up with. Save another dance for me and we'll find a dark corner to pick up where we left off.' He walked off chuckling, leaving an empty silence behind him.

The music struck up again and Rebecca's whole body tensed painfully. She glanced around almost desperately for Kym or Jock. For anyone.

'I . . . I'll just go and see that Tammy's all right,' she began breathily.

'Tammy's fine. She's having a great time,' he told her drily.

She couldn't stop her eyes slowly rising to meet his, and she immediately lost what breath she'd regained.

'Let's dance,' he said softly, and firmly pulled her into his arms.

Rebecca's legs felt like lead as she woodenly followed his lead. Her muscles ached with her rising tension.

'Just relax,' he said, his breath stirring the hair at her temples. 'Imagine you're still dancing with Kelly, if it'll help.'

Rebecca's chin jerked upwards so that she could look at him, and her anger rose. She'd already explained about her relationship with Davie Kelly.

'Look, Byron, I don't think we need to pander to convention by putting ourselves through the fiasco of dancing together.'

'I thought convention bothered you.' He held her closer, not allowing her to escape.

'What do you mean?'

'Weren't you worried about staying in the house alone with me? Both of us unmarried and unchaperoned; what would people say?' he mocked quietly.

'I'd like to sit down,' Rebecca got out icily. 'I see no point in continuing this dance or the conversation.'

'But I'm enjoying it, Becca, holding you close, smelling that perfume you're wearing. It could go to a man's head.' His hand moved slightly on her back, fingers teasing her through the soft material of her dress. 'Kelly seemed to be enjoying it, too.'

'He said he was,' Rebecca threw back at him. 'And you're being pretty childish, don't you think?'

His sharp, mirthless laugh stirred the hair over her ear and her senses tingled, threatened to abate her anger.

'I feel childish,' he bit out, and drew her impossibly closer to the unyielding contours of his hard body. 'And so bloody jealous I could make mincemeat of your old friend Kelly.'

Byron's legs moved against hers, stirred a spiral of wanting inside her. He had removed his jacket; her breasts brushed the silky material moulding his broad chest and her nipples throbbed, intensifying her need, sapping her strength, so that she sank against him.

'Davie's not——' She stopped, her voice catching in her dry mouth. She looked up into his face, meeting his gaze, and her rubbery legs almost gave way on her. He didn't even try to disguise the burning fire aglow in the blue-black pools of his eyes.

'Oh, Byron,' she sighed huskily. 'I——'

He swore softly under his breath. 'Just dance, Becca,' he said thickly, and gradually she let herself do just that.

It was a moment out of time for her. How she wished the dance could continue for ever, that she could go on floating in Byron's arms, feeling her body moulded to his, the movement of his hard thighs against hers, his hand slowly caressing her hip, her fingers resting lightly along the strong column of his throat. She could almost believe their heartbeats thudded in unison.

When the band stopped playing they continued to move to their own music for some seconds before they realised the other couples were leaving the floor. Caught up in the timeless euphoria, Rebecca sighed blissfully as she gazed up at him. His eyelashes fell then, shielding his expression, but she saw the pulse beating at the corner of his mouth.

He closed his eyes and expelled the breath he was holding. When he opened his eyes again he seemed to have himself under control, for he stepped away from her and motioned her to precede him from the floor.

Kym materialised from nowhere and grinned appealingly at Rebecca. 'Next one's mine,' he told her, and sat himself down beside her as she sank on to a chair. Not looking at her, Byron excused himself and walked off towards the group of men, all deep in conversation, gathered at one end of the hall.

For the rest of the evening Rebecca didn't lack dance partners. She danced with Kym, Jock and young men she'd known all her life growing up on the island. She could almost believe she'd never been away. Until she felt Byron's brooding gaze on her. She saw him take the floor with a number of different women, young and old, but he didn't seek her out again. By the time the dance wound up her heart was aching in her breast, and she had to force herself to smile her goodbyes to everyone as they headed for their cars to drive home.

Next day they were all strangely subdued, resting after their late night. On Monday, Byron dropped Kym down at Davie's boat, and when he returned to Bay Ridge he followed Jock out to the west paddock. Rebecca took Tammy into the garden to play until the increasing gusts of wind sent them inside.

'I don't think Davie would have taken the boat out in this, would he?' Rebecca asked Jock later in the afternoon.

'Depends where he was heading.' Jock chuckled. 'I hope Kym has his sea legs, though, because I've a feeling the lad'll need them.' When he saw Rebecca's frown, he patted her shoulder. 'Don't you go worrying. Davie's not foolhardy. He knows the sea and the weather. He won't do anything stupid.'

Lying in bed that night, listening to the wind howling around the house, Rebecca hoped Jock was right. She was still awake when the phone began to peal, and she sprang out of bed, dragging her eiderdown about her shoulders as she hurried into the living-room, half tripping over the trailing ends.

'Hello.' She almost dropped the receiver in her agitation. 'Bay Ridge.'

'Is Will there?' asked a deep voice.

'Yes. Just a minute. I'll get him.' She turned as Byron came into the room. 'It's for you.' She held out the handpiece, her eyes large in her face.

'Byron Willoughby,' he said and then listened, turning his back slightly so that Rebecca couldn't see his face. 'Right. I'll be ready. I'll meet you at the gate.'

'What's happened?' Rebecca asked apprehensively as he replaced the receiver.

'It's the *Kelly Two*. They've been in a spot of trouble and she's taking water fast,' he told her flatly.

'Oh, no!' Rebecca breathed, as an icy hand of fear clutched at her.

'Davie radioed that they'd managed to get back into the lee of the island, but he's not sure that the pumps can handle the water. He's going to try to beach the boat.' Byron frowned and then moved towards his room. 'I'd better get dressed. Davie's father and brother are picking me up, and we're going down there.'

Rebecca stood in the hallway, shivering beneath the eiderdown, and in no time Byron was back wearing jeans and a thick sweater. He carried his waterproof jacket, and he paused when he saw her standing there. His face grew even more strained.

'Try not to worry, Becca,' he said softly, and she nodded.

Their eyes met, held, and Byron was the first to turn away, to hurry outside to the shed. Moments later his car sped out towards the road.

Rebecca slowly forced herself to move. There was no point in returning to bed, for she'd never sleep, so she dressed in warm slacks and a jumper and went into the kitchen to brew some tea. Not that she felt like drinking it, but it was something to do. And it was a long night.

When the phone eventually rang she sped to answer it with something akin to terror in her heart. She almost fainted with relief when Byron told her all was well and that he was about to leave for home, bringing Kym with him.

It seemed that the *Kelly Two* had moved past the tip of Cape Borda and been hit by large swells from the south-west. One abnormally high swell had done the damage, taking them unawares, carrying the boat upwards like a piece of driftwood, only to drop it down the other side of the wave into a deep, steep, shallow trough. The impact had holed the bow, and the boat had begun taking water. But thankfully Davie had managed to limp back to the sheltered side of the island and they were all safely ashore now.

Rebecca carried the cup of hot soup into Kym's room. He was sitting propped up against a couple of pillows and he smiled at her as she handed him the steaming liquid. He took a sip.

'Ah. That's great, Becca. Thanks.' He drank some more and then set the mug down on the bedside table.

'Feeling better?' she asked, and he nodded.

'It's good to be warm again. The cold was the worst part.'

Rebecca sat down on the side of the bed and, taking his chin in her fingers, she turned the side of his face to the dawning light that was glowing in the window.

'You're going to have a pretty impressive shiner,' she teased him.

Kym grimaced. 'That was my own fault. I tripped over my own feet. Talk about awkward! But I wouldn't have missed it, Becca,' he added earnestly. 'Even when I was terrified out of my wits, I wouldn't have wanted to miss it.'

'That I don't understand,' Rebecca remarked with feeling.

'No, honestly, Becca. It's funny, but I can see a lot of things more clearly now. In those split seconds when we hung on that wave, I remember thinking, "This can't be the end, I haven't done anything with my life yet." And I thought about that afterwards when we were waiting for help to come. I've been wasting this year, Becca. I knew what I wanted to do, but I was too damn lazy and maybe a little scared to do it.'

'Oh, I think you were entitled to take time to make a decision that affected your future.' Rebecca patted his hand and his fingers clasped hers lightly.

'No, I was just making excuses for myself. Like getting angry at Byron because he'd been so successful and didn't need to prove anything anymore. That kind of stuff.' He sighed heavily. 'I knew I'd never be the footballer my brother was, and I sort of held that against him, even though I didn't really want to play footie. I was so damn mixed up. But not now, Becca. Although I'm sorry about Davie's boat, I'm really glad this has happened to get me together. Bit selfish, eh?'

'Very.' Rebecca agreed teasingly. 'And what are you going to do?' she asked.

'See if I can get into marine biology. I've always been interested in it. Maybe up in Queensland at Townsville Uni.' He sighed and then frowned seriously. 'I didn't realise Byron would be so worried about me. He was, wasn't he?'

Rebecca nodded.

'I'd like to see him happy, Becca,' he said slowly. 'And you, too. Maybe together, hmm?'

'Kym——' she began warningly, and he held up his hand.

'OK. None of my business. What am I? A self-centred, egotistical little pain in the butt?' He laughed and Rebecca laughed with him.

'Something like that.' She shook her head. 'I'm glad you're OK.' Putting her arms around him, she hugged him tightly.

'Wow! Here's another reason why I'm glad this happened.' He put his arms around her and kissed her noisily on the cheek. 'You know, if you ever lose your position here at Bay Ridge, I've heard Townsville's not a bad place. I could show you a great time, kid,' he chuckled softly in her ear, and she laughed with him.

'It would serve you right if I accepted that proposition, Kym Willoughby.' She moved back to look at him, her arms still loosely around him.

'Promises, promises,' laughed Kym. 'Oh, hi, Byron,' he said over her shoulder and Rebecca tensed, moving away from him and standing up.

Slowly she turned to face the doorway. Byron had showered and shaved, but his face still bore witness to his anxious night. His eyes speared coldly over her, his mouth twisting, and she could guess just what he was thinking. *Now I find you in my young brother's arms.*

She bit her lip as a rush of tears flooded her eyes, and she brushed past him, not caring where she was going, only knowing she had had enough, that she had to get away from him. He called her name, but she ignored it as she raced through the kitchen and out into the yard, not stopping until she reached the grove of king mallees. Breathlessly she sank down on to the old seat she and Rudy had made out of planks, and the tears poured down her face.

'Becca.' His hand reached out to touch her, drew her to her feet and into his arms, holding her close against the musky warmth of him until her sobs ceased.

'I'm sorry,' she mumbled at last.

'So am I,' he said thickly. 'For being such a bloody-minded fool. I've been taking out my frustrations on you because you turned me down when you had every right to do so.'

He stood away from her and drew a ragged breath. 'My only excuse, if you'll accept one, is that I love you so much, I couldn't bear thinking of you with anyone else or of my life without you.'

Rebecca stared up at him and slowly shook her head, half laughing, half crying. 'Oh, Byron! I love you, too. So very much.' She threw herself back into his arms and they clung together until Byron leant back to gaze down into her eyes.

'Then why on earth did you say you wouldn't marry me?' he asked huskily.

'Because you never once mentioned love. You just said you wanted me,' she told him. 'But never that you loved me.'

'Women!' His appeal went skywards. 'I thought actions spoke louder than mere words. And as for words, it's a wonder I could even speak coherently that night. You had me so tied up in knots, I didn't know if I was right side up or not. How could you doubt I loved you to distraction?'

'I thought——' Rebecca paused and he raised one dark eyebrow. 'I thought you could only love Tammy's mother,' she finished quickly. 'You said she was the most beautiful woman you'd ever seen.'

Byron sat down on the bench and pulled Rebecca on to his knee. 'Becca, that part of my life is behind me, and I'm glad you didn't know me then.' His eyes looked off into the distance, although his thumb absently caressed her hand.

'I'd been playing football all my life, it seemed, and I guess I started to believe what I read about myself in the papers. I began to think I *was* some kind of god. I married Nikki because, well, I saw her as the right kind of wife. For the King of Carlton.' His lips twisted self-derisively. 'She was beautiful, everyone envied me, and I couldn't see past that beauty. I was in love with the wrapping, not the cold, selfish personality underneath. Perhaps I didn't want to see it. Maybe it was enough that she fitted the image I wanted at the time.

'But of course, everyone has to come down to earth eventually, and when I did, it was to the realisation that I'd married an empty, shallow shell. By then, we had Tammy and our marriage was virtually over. Nikki didn't care for motherhood. It was too restricting, spoilt her figure, interfered with her life-style. And I was too busy playing the crowd's idol to realise, or even care, what Nikki was doing.'

Rebecca lifted his hand and placed a soft kiss on his palm.

Byron's eyes burned down into hers. 'Oh, Becca, I don't deserve you.' His eyes fell from hers.

'Byron——' she began, but he put one finger on her lips.

'Let me finish, Becca. I don't want any shadows rearing out of the past.' He grimaced. 'I have to admit that the break-up of our marriage wasn't all Nikki's fault. It was partly mine, too, because I made no effort whatsoever to try to mend the break. Anyway, when I had the operation on my knee it gave me time to think about my life, and I didn't like what I saw. Nikki and I were finished, we both knew that. She found a new football hero, a friend of mine who played for Carlton. Afterwards I tried to get my interest back in the game, in the life I'd been leading, but it had gone sour on me. I had to get out. And I owed Tammy a better life than the one she'd had till then.'

He sighed. 'Meeting Rudy when I was over in Port Lincoln, visiting Laurel and Bill, and hearing that Jock was thinking of selling the farm was a heaven-sent opportunity. So I came here to the island and Bay Ridge. And I found that buried treasure you were talking about. You, my love.' He kissed her with lingering tenderness. 'I love you, and you only, Rebecca Grainger,' he said sincerely. 'I think I did right from the moment you threw yourself into my arms.'

'You did?' she laughed a little breathlessly. 'It was too dark to even see me properly.'

'But I could feel you, and I thought, "As of now, this is one of Rudy's *ex*-girlfriends, because this one's going to be mine."' He pulled a face. 'I was scared stiff you wouldn't take the job I offered you, and what with Jock playing matchmaker so blatantly, I wasn't sure how hard to press you to stay. I planned on sweeping you off your feet, you see. Only you didn't exactly fall into my arms, did you?'

Rebecca shook her head. 'I wanted to, but I suppose I was a little frightened by the way you made me feel.'

'I was a trifle overbearing at times, wasn't I? God, Becca, I was out of control. I couldn't seem to do or say the right things to you. When everyone started pairing us off and you kept denying it so firmly I wanted to——' He shook his head. 'I didn't know whether to shake you or make love to you.'

Rebecca swallowed unsteadily. 'I probably deserved the shaking. I did say some terrible things to you, didn't I?'

He kissed her again. 'You surely did. Not to mention turning me down and then proceeding to bring your old boyfriends to light. I was about ready to tear Kelly apart limb by limb. And Kym,' he added with feeling.

'I don't think you need to worry about Kym. He's sorted himself out very nicely.' Rebecca chuckled and then sobered. 'I'm sorry about Davie, though. He...you see Jock and Davie's parents thought we should get married, and I wasn't going to be forced into it because I didn't love him.' She sighed. 'That's why I left the island, because Jock was trying to pair me off with Davie.'

'Ah, Davie Kelly,' Byron said ominously. 'When I came in and found him kissing you I——' he shook his head '—I was so damn jealous I could have torn him away from you and thrown him out of the house. And when you carefully implied we were more than friends, I very nearly picked you up and carted you off to my bed.'

'I probably would have only put up a token resistance.' Rebecca's laugh was shakily emotive. 'Anyway,' she drew a steadying breath, 'Davie didn't want to marry me any more than I wanted to marry him. As a matter of fact,' she ran her hand lightly over the bulge of muscle in his forearm, 'he thought I was frigid.'

Byron raised his eyebrows. 'He must be mad,' he said with feeling.

'I was never interested in him romantically, not then and not now. Especially now,' she added huskily, and trailed a fingertip down his freshly shaven cheek to trace the line of his lips.

Byron drew a sharp breath and crushed her to him, kissing her desperately with a passion she matched. When they drew apart they were breathless.

'We'd better draw the line at that,' he remarked unsteadily, 'or Jock will be coming after me with a shotgun.' He smiled. 'Let's go home.' Byron stood up, letting her slide slowly down his hard body, until her feet touched the ground. 'Jock sure knew what he was doing when he decided to show off his beautiful granddaughter.'

Rebecca grimaced. 'When I realised what he'd done, I was so embarrassed I could have died.'

'God, Becca, when you turned me down I very nearly——' He held her tightly to him for long, impassioned moments before gradually relaxing his hold to gaze down at her. 'At the risk of repeating myself, Miss Grainger,' he said formally, his voice still slightly unsteady, 'I think we'd better get married, and pretty damn quickly.'

And this time Rebecca agreed that perhaps it might be best.

Janet BAILEY

THE MASTER FIDDLER

Jacqui didn't want to go back to college, and she didn't want to go home. Tombstone, Arizona, wasn't in her plans, either, until she found herself stuck there en route to L.A. after ramming her car into rancher Choya Barnett's Jeep. Things got worse when she lost her wallet and couldn't pay for the repairs. The mechanic wasn't interested when she practically propositioned him to get her car back—but Choya was. He took care of her bills and then waited for the debt to be paid with the only thing Jacqui had to offer—her virtue.

Watch for this bestselling Janet Dailey favorite, coming in June from Harlequin.

Also watch for *Something Extra* in August and *Sweet Promise* in October.

You'll flip . . . your pages won't!
Read paperbacks *hands-free* with

Book Mate · I

The perfect "mate" for all your romance paperbacks
Traveling • Vacationing • At Work • In Bed • Studying
• Cooking • Eating

Perfect size for all standard paperbacks, this wonderful invention makes reading a pure pleasure! Ingenious design holds paperback books OPEN and FLAT so even wind can't ruffle pages — leaves your hands free to do other things. Reinforced, wipe-clean vinyl-covered holder flexes to let you turn pages without undoing the strap . . . supports paperbacks so well, they have the strength of hardcovers!

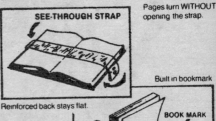

Pages turn WITHOUT opening the strap.

SEE-THROUGH STRAP

Reinforced back stays flat.

Built in bookmark

BOOK MARK

BACK COVER HOLDING STRIP

10 x 7¼ . opened.
Snaps closed for easy carrying, too